Children's Literature Merit Award
—Midwest Independent Publishers Association

"Wonderfully written and a joy to read."
—*Midwest Book Review*

"Fascinating . . . like a modern-day version of Lewis Carroll's *Alice's Adventures in Wonderland.*"
—*Mathematics Teacher*

A GEBRA NAMED AL

A GEBRA NAMED AL

A Novel by Wendy Isdell

Edited by Pamela Espeland

free spirit
PUBLISHING®
Helping kids
help themselves™
since 1983

Library of Congress Cataloging-in-Publication Data

Isdell, Wendy, 1975–

A gebra named Al / by Wendy Isdell ; edited by Pamela Espeland.

p. cm.

Summary: Trouble with her algebra homework leads Julie through a mysterious portal into the Land of Mathematics, where a zebra-like creature and horses representing Periodic Elements help her learn about math and chemistry in order to get home.

ISBN 0-915793-58-X

[1. Fantasy. 2. Mathematics—Fiction. 3. Chemistry—Fiction. 4. Youths' writings.] I. Espeland, Pamela. II. Title.

PZ7.I772Ge 1993

[Fic]—dc20 93-15294

CIP

AC

Cover and map illustration by David Kacmarynski

Map created by Wendy Isdell

20 19 18 17 16 15 14 13

Printed in Canada

Free Spirit Publishing Inc.

217 Fifth Avenue North, Suite 200

Minneapolis, MN 55401-1299

(612) 338-2068

help4kids@freespirit.com

www.freespirit.com

Dedication

To Jerion, the Imaginary Number
and also to Mrs. Garrison, Mrs. Stone, and
Mrs. Balgavy, from eighth grade; Mrs. Clark and
the FOCUS program; and all others who aided me
in this prodigious project.

Contents

Map of Mathematics viii

Who's Who in *A Gebra Named Al* x

Chapter 1: Julie Gets a Wrong Answer 1

Chapter 2: The Periodics Appear 11

Chapter 3: The Council in the Clearing 23

Chapter 4: The Orders of Operations 34

Chapter 5: Between Multiplication and Division 46

Chapter 6: The Path around Addition Mountain 57

Chapter 7: The Wolframs Attack 68

Chapter 8: At the Mathematician's Castle 78

Chapter 9: Julie Goes Home 87

About the Author 97

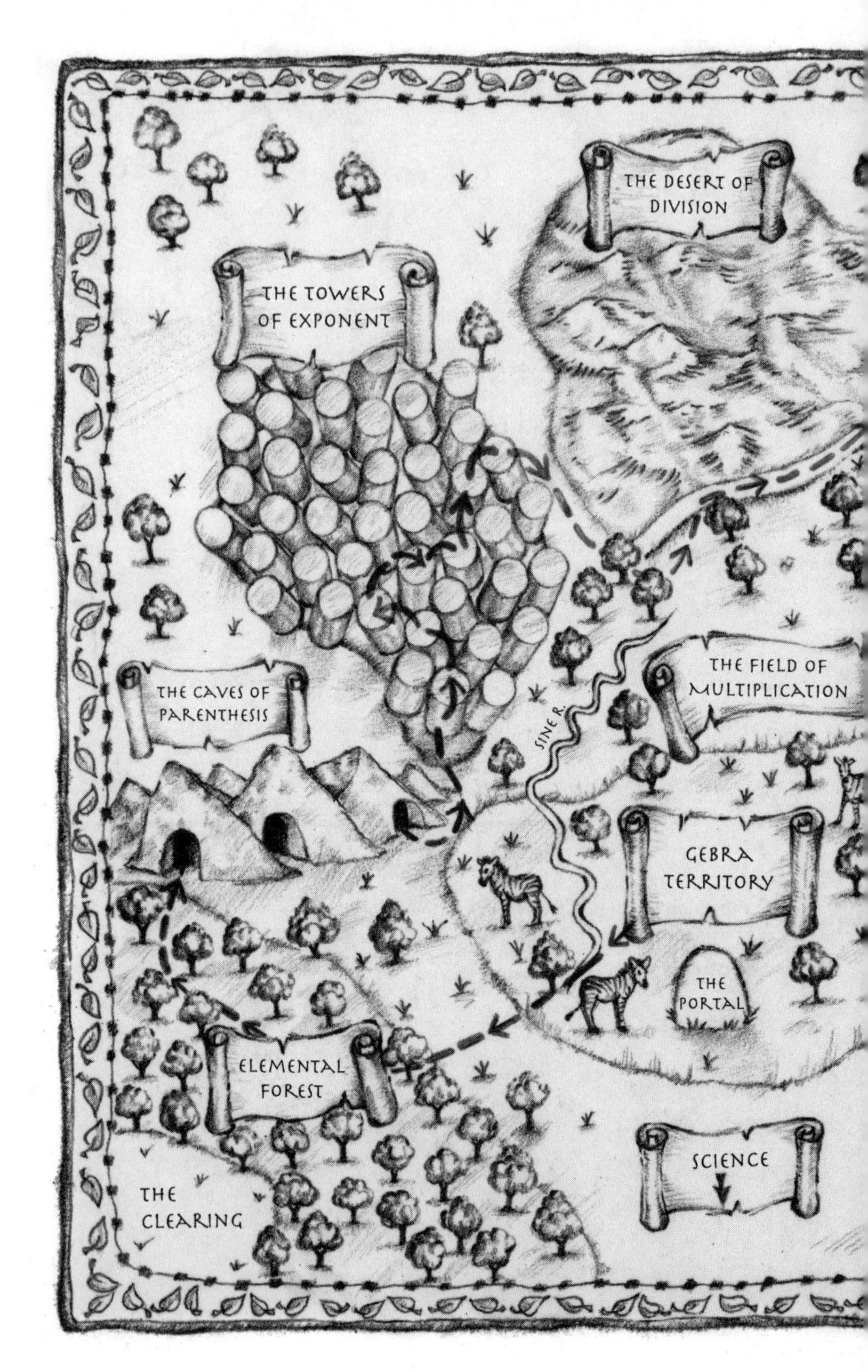
THE DESERT OF DIVISION
THE TOWERS OF EXPONENT
THE FIELD OF MULTIPLICATION
THE CAVES OF PARENTHESIS
SINE R.
GEBRA TERRITORY
THE PORTAL
ELEMENTAL FOREST
SCIENCE
THE CLEARING

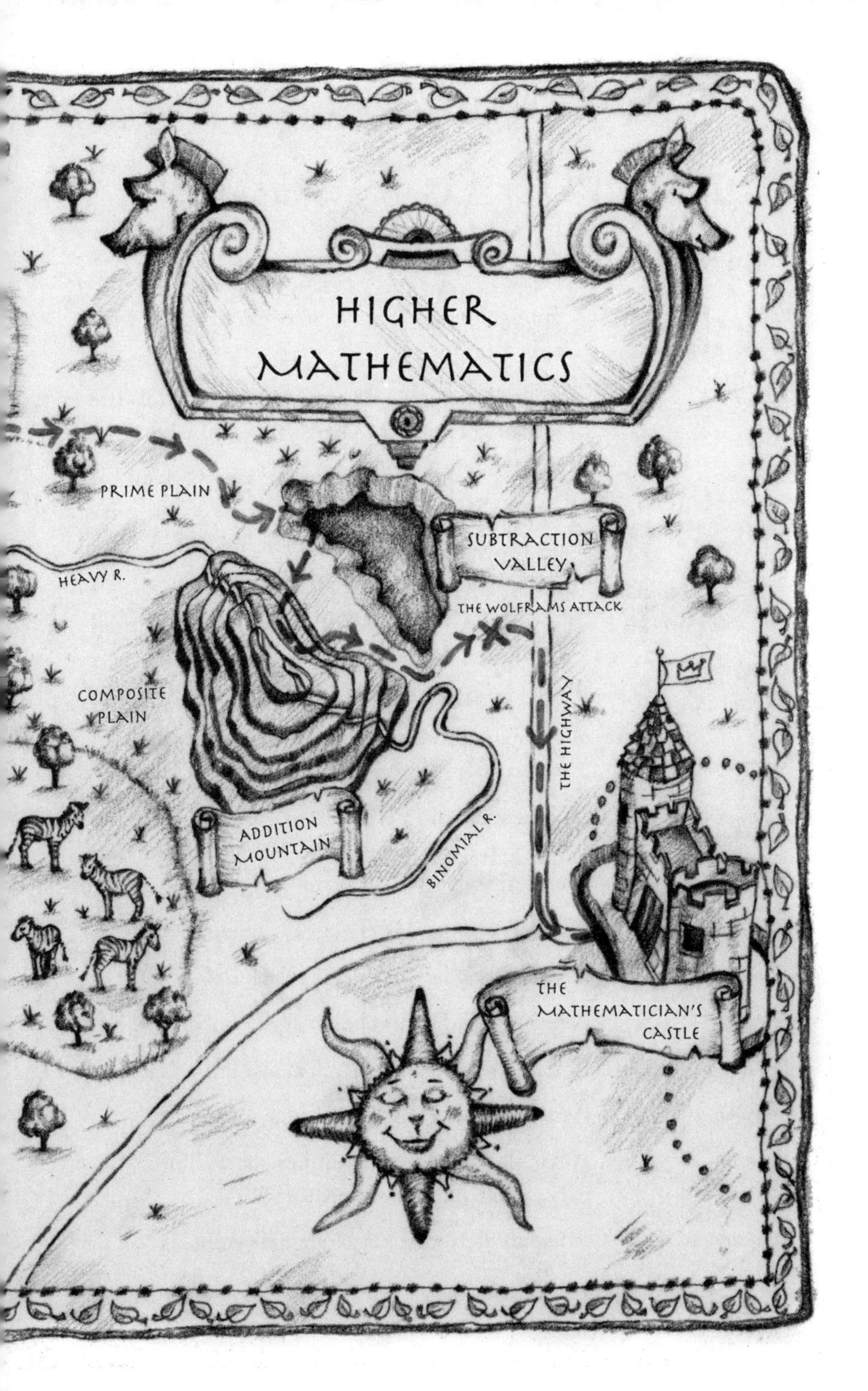
HIGHER MATHEMATICS
PRIME PLAIN
SUBTRACTION VALLEY
HEAVY R.
THE WOLFRAMS ATTACK
COMPOSITE PLAIN
THE HIGHWAY
ADDITION MOUNTAIN
BINOMIAL R.
THE MATHEMATICIAN'S CASTLE

Who's Who in A Gebra Named Al

In order of appearance:

Julie	A young human female who has trouble with her algebra
Jerion	A male Imaginary Number, emissary of the Mathematician, sent to help young humans
Al	A gebra; Julie's first friend in the land of Mathematics, and a member of the group that takes her to the Mathematician; his "stripes" are actually long lines of equations
The Main Gebra	The massive leader of the gebra herd; printed across his chest is the equation $E = mc^2$
Lithium	A male Periodic, Al's best friend, and a member of the group that takes Julie to the Mathematician; his chemical symbol is "Li"
Hydrogen	A silvery female Periodic, and a member of the group that takes Julie to the Mathematician; her chemical symbol is "H"
Cesium	A male Periodic; his chemical symbol is "Cs"
Francium	A male Periodic; his chemical symbol is "Fr"
Sodium	A male Periodic; his chemical symbol is "Na"
Rubidium	A male Periodic; his chemical symbol is "Rb"
Potassium	A male Periodic; his chemical symbol is "K"
Kalium	A female Isotope; Potassium's sister; her chemical symbol, like Potassium's, is "K"
Oxygen	A female Periodic; her chemical symbol is "O"

Deuterium	A male Isotope, and a member of the group that takes Julie to the Mathematician; Hydrogen's brother; his chemical symbol is "${}^{2}_{1}H$"
Tritium	A male Isotope, and a member of the group that takes Julie to the Mathematician; Hydrogen's brother; his chemical symbol is "${}^{3}_{1}H$"
The Wolframs	Dangerous servants of the power-hungry Periodic, Tungsten; sometimes they look like shaggy brown wolves, at other times like large, powerful rams
Mark Carscian	An adult human male, and an official representative of the Mathematician
Mark's Horse	The image of a horse; actually an Imaginary Number
The Gatekeeper	A talkative male guard at the Mathematician's Castle
The Mathematician	The ruler of the land of Mathematics; a tiny, kind-hearted, white-bearded man who wears a simple crown
Bromius	A male Imaginary Number at the court of the Mathematician

1

Julie Gets a Wrong Answer

JULIE SIGHED AS SHE STARED OUT THE WINDOW AT THE pouring rain. She was trying to think of a topic to write a story about. Her wrist was hurting from forty-five minutes of supporting her head, so she dropped her pencil disconsolately and straightened in her chair, taking the weight off the aching joint. The clock on her desk said 4:30. Her parents wouldn't be home from work for another two hours, and her little brother was visiting a friend. She was alone in the house.

"I might as well do my homework," she sighed. The fantasy story she was writing for a school contest just wasn't working out. Normally she loved to write, but today for some reason she had writer's block. She shoved the folder for her story aside and took her algebra book out of her book bag.

"Page 56," she noted out loud, glancing at her memo notebook. She opened the algebra book to page 56 and lifted out the paper lodged between the pages. It was the one on which she had started the assignment earlier that afternoon.

"Negative five plus three times six," she said. She computed the answer, then turned to the back of the book to check the answer key. Her answer was wrong.

With a sigh of frustration, Julie read the problem again. "$-5 + 3(6)$," it said, exactly as it had before. And earlier that afternoon, too, in class. So why did she keep getting it wrong?

"What's wrong with my answer?" she growled. Negative five plus three was negative two; negative two times six was negative twelve. Why did the book give the answer as positive thirteen?

She worked on the problem for a few more minutes, but finally gave up in exasperation. She buried her head in her arms over the book and closed her eyes. She hated algebra! She just didn't understand it. Soon she fell asleep with her head on the book, and in her sleep she began to dream.

$$\{3^{[3+(2\times 6)]}\}+[4(13-6)]=$$

She was in space—deep, black space, but there were no stars. Instead, she saw long streaks of light, stretching across the sky and all around her. Light green, purple, and magenta laser beams reached as far as she could see, out from a point behind her to a point so far ahead that her mind balked when she tried to fathom it.

"Negative five plus three times six is negative twelve!" Julie screamed into the blackness.

Thirteen, thirteen, came a soft whisper from everywhere at once.

She jumped, looking around, but there was no one. So she got even angrier. "Negative five plus three is negative two!" she shouted. "Negative two times six is negative twelve!"

Parenthesis, exponent, multiplication, division, addition, subtraction, recited the haunting whisper. *You should have multiplied first. Three times six is eighteen. Negative five plus eighteen is thirteen.*

Julie stopped, thinking it over. "You're right," she said. "That's the order of operations for algebraic equations. Parenthesis, exponent, multiplication, division, addition, subtraction—PEMDAS. And multiplication comes before addition, so . . . ." She shook her head and recalculated, this time getting the correct answer.

You really need help, remarked the voice conversationally.

"I really do," Julie agreed ruefully.

"Wake up," commanded the voice from directly behind her. Suddenly she was back in her room. She blinked, rubbing the sleep from her eyes, and heard the voice again: "Wake up!" Startled, Julie staggered to her feet, accidentally knocking her algebra book onto the floor.

"Pick it up." The voice was normal now, and soft, but definitely behind her.

Julie turned quickly, but she couldn't see anything but the white plaster wall, her bed with the rumpled blue unicorn covers, and her huge teddy bear.

"Where are you?" she called, puzzled.

"Pick up the book," repeated the soft voice.

Grimacing, she bent, carefully, and retrieved the heavy schoolbook.

"Now look."

Julie looked behind her again and saw a dark portal, as if someone had smeared a big inkblot on the air between her bed and herself. In front of the portal floated a white, almost translucent cloud. The bottom of the cloud just barely brushed the floor, and it was not quite as high as the portal.

"Who are you?" she inquired. Was the cloud talking to her, or was someone or something else hidden behind the cloud?

"I am an Imaginary Number, an emissary of the Mathematician," replied the voice. It seemed to be coming from the cloud after all.

"What are you doing in my room?" Julie demanded, not even trying to figure out what the Imaginary Number had just told her.

"I'm not really in your room. I reside behind the book."

Julie looked skeptically at the book in her arms. "The book?"

"The book," affirmed the Imaginary Number, nodding his vaguely spherical top portion, which Julie decided was his head.

"This book," stated Julie doubtfully.

"No other than."

"Who in the world would want to live in an algebra book, much less my algebra book?"

"I'm actually *behind* the book," responded the Imaginary Number. "Just don't worry about it."

"Well, why are you in my room?" Julie insisted.

"I can see that you definitely need some help with math, young girl. I just stopped by to see how anyone could actually be so bad at it."

"How do you know?" bridled Julie. "That I'm bad at it, I mean?" She didn't like numbers in the first place, and this one, imaginary or not, wasn't turning out to be any better than the others. At least the others hadn't insulted her.

"When you fell asleep over the algebra book, your mind entered a portal to my land. That happens sometimes when the conditions are right. Anyway, I saw you and heard you yelling out that horribly incorrect answer to a relatively simple problem. That's how I know." The Imaginary Number floated closer, and Julie looked at him suspiciously.

"Your land?" she asked.

The Number pointed behind himself with one white extremity much like a hand. "This portal opens up to it."

"What is your land?"

"My land is a land of math. There Imaginary Numbers are real beings"—here the cloud bent in the middle, as if bowing—

"and numerical animals roam at will. Perhaps you'd like to call my land 'Mathematics.' It's a simple enough name." The Number's tone seemed to imply that was reason enough for Julie to use it. "Our ruler is called the Mathematician."

"The Mathematician," Julie repeated. She was skeptical.

"The Mathematician," the Number assured her.

Suddenly Julie was angry. This whole thing was a joke someone was playing on her! It had to be. "I hate math," she declared. "And I'm not sure I like you, either, whatever you are and wherever you come from."

The Imaginary Number looked mortally insulted. "Look, Human female," he told her, "I don't *have* to come to this place, seek out young Humans like yourself, and give them support. I could ask the Mathematician for another assignment! Come to think of it, I believe I will . . . ." The Imaginary Number's lecture abruptly drifted off. "Never mind," he said briskly. "It's time for me to leave. I have other matters to attend to." The Number swiveled and drifted purposefully toward the portal.

"Wait!" cried Julie. This *thing* had suddenly appeared, criticized her, and was leaving without even a farewell! Even if this whole scene was a joke someone was playing on her, nobody got away with that! In her anger, Julie did not even pause to wonder how the joker could have put a portal in the middle of her room.

"Come back!" she shouted. She ran after the rapidly disappearing white cloud, which was already halfway through the portal. She hit the portal at a dead run and was instantly through, with only the tiniest glimpse of the green-and-purple-streaked black space she had seen in her dream.

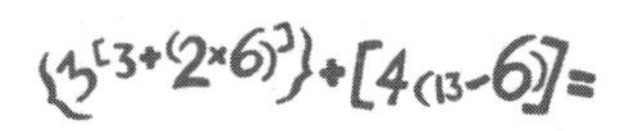

She was in a field. A big, green, open field. She blinked, trying to look around her, but the bright light almost blinded her after the dimness of her room. She could smell great expanses of grass and clover. Amazed, she peered into the featureless greenness all around her, waiting impatiently for her eyes to adjust. When she could finally see, she sighted a small herd of animals on the horizon. They were striped in black-and-white and looked a lot like horses.

"Zebras!" she exclaimed. Forgetting all about algebra, the Imaginary Number, the Mathematician, and her room, Julie ran toward the zebras, delighted. She loved animals with a passion, especially horses, and she knew that zebras belonged to the horse family.

One of the zebras raised its head at her approach and snorted loudly. Julie could hear it even from several hundred feet away. She expected to see the whole herd take off in fright, like they did in the wildlife shows on TV whenever intruders came too near, but to her surprise only the one zebra moved—toward her, coming at a gallop.

She froze in terror as the animal bore down on her. His massive hooves churned up the grass and soil as his bulging muscles propelled him toward her at tremendous speed. A voice in her mind tried to reassure her that it only *looked* like he was traveling a hundred miles per hour—no zebra could go *that* fast—but this was no time to think rationally. Julie knew she should run, but she was so frightened she couldn't move. Instead, she stood paralyzed until the zebra was almost on top of her. He braked abruptly only a few feet away.

"Hello!" he exclaimed.

Julie blinked. "What?"

The zebra put back his ears and opened his nostrils to whiff the air.

"I said, 'Hello.' Can you hear?" The zebra paused for a moment, tilting his head slightly. "Or perhaps you are unable to hear?"

Julie shook her head. Maddeningly, the theme song from "Mr. Ed," an old TV series about a talking horse, was going around inside her head.

"Yes, I can hear. I just didn't know zebras could talk."

The zebra swished his tail, shifted his weight, and eyed her. "Well, we can," he said. His voice was that of a young man. "And you pronounced it wrong," he added. "It's 'gebra,' not 'zebra.'"

"Jeebra?" Julie repeated, staring. Now she saw that the black stripes on the animal's short white fur—which originally had led her to believe he was a zebra—were actually long equations arranged in stripes.

The gebra's ears spread wide. "Yes, gebra!" it exclaimed. "Spelled g-e-b-r-a. Now, hop on; I'll take you to the Main Gebra, and the fastest way is for you to ride on my back. You need help!"

That reminded Julie of the Imaginary Number. Briefly she wondered what had happened to him, but since he obviously wasn't here she dismissed the thought. Besides, the gebra was already three times more help than the Number had been.

She went up to the gebra, whose back was at the level of her chest, and took a handful of mane. She hoped it didn't hurt him too much to pull on it, but the gebra did not wince or move as she grabbed hold. She tried to swing her leg up on his back, but she couldn't reach it. Then she tried to haul herself up by the handful of mane, but that was too difficult.

"Hurry," urged the gebra, turning his head to nudge her leg with his nose.

"You're too high," she protested, trying to jump up again.

"Oh, of course—sorry." The gebra slowly lowered himself down to the ground until he was kneeling in front of her. "How about now?"

"Good," Julie approved, swinging her leg over his back at last and finding a seat. The gebra rose to his feet with a surge, and Julie found herself perched precariously on the creature's bony, fuzzy back.

The gebra shook his mane, almost dislodging her, and moved off at a fast trot.

"No! No! At a walk!" cried Julie, her legs wrapped desperately around the gebra's shoulders. She had never ridden a gebra before, or a horse, for that matter.

The gebra slowed to a walk, his ears pressed back in annoyance. "We'll never get there at this rate," he complained.

When they had traveled across the warm, sunny field for a few minutes, slowly drawing closer to the peacefully grazing gebra herd, Julie leaned forward a bit and asked, "What's your name, gebra?"

The gebra's ears went up. "Al," he replied. "Al Gebra."

"Al Gebra," repeated Julie slowly. Al had pronounced the word like "JEE-bra," and the long "e" ruined the pun. "Is it 'jee-bra' or 'jeh-bra?'" she asked, wanting to make sure.

"It's either," answered the gebra, bouncing along. He sniffed a tall pink flower as they passed it, then swished his tail so the black tassel on the end stung Julie's skin. "And what is your name?"

"Julie," she replied. "Who is the Main Gebra?"

"He runs the herd," returned Al. "He tells us what to do. Julie . . . . That's an interesting name."

"Like the stallion in a herd of horses?" pressed Julie, not intentionally ignoring the comment about her name. She was just overwhelmed with curiosity, and her name was irrelevant compared to this new and fascinating world.

"What's a horse?" inquired Al.

Julie relaxed and sat back, then immediately stiffened. What if she fell off? This wasn't the time to relax. "A horse is like you, but with no equations."

"No equations?" The gebra sounded outraged. "How horrible!" A shudder went through him, rippling the skin underneath Julie. She suddenly wished she had a saddle.

"And also," she continued, "a horse's tail is long and stringy, not like a long, skinny, furry tube with a tassel on the end." As Julie described the gebra's tail, it flicked again, slapping against her back.

"Horses are brown and black and red and golden," she stated.

"Multicolored, eh?" commented Al.

"No!" exclaimed Julie. "There are many different kinds. Mostly they are one color."

"Do they look like us?" remarked Al. "Our closest relatives are the Periodics and the Isotopes. They resemble the creatures you call 'horses,' except they are most often silver or gray."

"Periodics? Isotopes?"

"Yep." Al nodded his head, glancing back at her. That was easy to do, since his eyes were almost on the sides of his head. He simply had to angle his head a bit to one side, and Julie was staring him right in one brown eye. But Al kept his eyes mainly forward while he walked.

Soon they had reached the edge of the herd and were working their way inward past hundreds of gebras which paid them little or no attention.

"One of my best friends is Lithium," Al told her, dodging a young gebra which cavorted into their path and kept going.

Julie turned her attention from the little gebra back to Al's fuzzy ears. "Lithium?" she asked. The word struck a bell, but Julie couldn't make the connection.

"Yeah, you know, Lithium. A Periodic. As in the Alkali Metals?" Al nodded his head, dodged around a small throng of gebras, and stopped suddenly before a massive gebra. Across his chest was printed boldly:

$$\mathbf{E = mc^2}$$

2

The Periodics Appear

THE MAIN GEBRA STOOD MUCH TALLER THAN AL AND had an aura of power. This was definitely someone in charge. He looked down at Julie with something close to disdain and asked, "What is this?"

Julie sat up straight, held tightly to Al's mane, and answered, "My name is Julie. I'm a girl."

"Hmmmm." The Main Gebra sniffed her doubtfully. "You smell faintly Human," he muttered in his deep voice.

"Faintly?" Julie was puzzled. "I should smell a lot like a human! I am one."

"A Human!" exclaimed Al, his ears spread wide in amazement. "There is a Human on my back!" For some reason he sounded excited.

The Main Gebra looked Julie in the eye. "How may we help you, Human?" Suddenly, to Julie's surprise and embarrassment, he bowed low to the ground.

Julie was caught between the total unexpectedness of the bow, the strangeness of seeing any animal bow, and the question. "Er, well, the Imaginary Number said I needed to learn more about algebra," she finally began, for lack of anything else to say. By now Julie was getting uncomfortable on Al's back, and she squirmed—just a little, as the Main Gebra had risen from his bow and was looking at her again.

"Certainly," stated the Main Gebra. "Al can teach you easily."

The last thing Julie wanted was to have to do more algebra problems. "Uh, no, thank you," she politely declined. "Actually, well, I'd like to see you bow again." She giggled, startled at her own intrepidity.

The Main Gebra smiled (another strange thing for an animal to do) and humored her with a resigned air. This time Julie watched how he bent his front legs while keeping his back legs straight, and ducked his head down.

"That's good," Julie approved, clapping appreciatively.

The Main Gebra smiled tolerantly. "Why are you here?" he asked. "Very few Humans visit our herd."

"I don't really know," she admitted. "And I'm not really a visitor. I mean, I don't know how I got here, and I don't know how to get back." At this point, there was no question in her mind about whether this world was real or not—she was definitely here, and definitely stuck. The portal was missing, and so was the Imaginary Number.

"Back to your world? Back to the Place of Humans?" Al was shivering now. "Oh, I'd like to see it! All those Humans, grouped together! Imagine the power—"

"Al," growled the Main Gebra softly, interrupting him.

"Oh, yes. Sorry." Al stopped talking, but he still fidgeted with excitement, twitching his tail back and forth.

"Well, Human," resumed the Main Gebra thoughtfully, "I don't know any way for you to leave this world and return to your own. But perhaps one of the Periodics knows."

Al had used that word—Periodics. But what—or who—were the Periodics?

"You'll have to have someone to carry you, of course," continued the Main Gebra, casually glancing around at the herd. "The Periodic Council is meeting two days' distance from here.

And you'll need someone who knows them. They don't always welcome strangers." The Main Gebra gazed thoughtfully at Al.

"You mean I can carry the Human some more?" asked Al. "Hooray!" He started to jump around in excitement, almost shaking Julie off his back. She wondered what he was so happy about and crossly gave him a warning kick in the side. Al subsided.

"But, first, a saddle," said the Main Gebra wisely. He clicked his teeth resoundingly, and two more gebras approached and pointed their ears at the Main Gebra.

"Bring the saddle," commanded the Main Gebra. He looked at Julie and explained, "We keep one for those rare occasions when Humans grace us with their presence."

One hour later, with a leather saddle beneath her, complete with saddlebags, and a fine leather bridle strap in her hands, Julie set off to meet the Periodics, mounted on Al the gebra. As they rode across the warm green grass, Julie was overcome by a feeling of contentment, despite the fact that she was trapped in a strange world and didn't know how she would get home—or even if she could get home.

Her thoughts turned to the story she had been trying to write for her school contest.

"Hey, Al," she called toward the fuzzy ears, which rotated toward her in response.

"Yes?" returned the gebra, with a note of respect she had heard ever since the Main Gebra had identified her as a human.

"I'm trying to write a story. What do you think I should write about? It's going to be a fantasy story."

The gebra's gait became rough for a moment, as if he were frustrated. "I know only of mathematics," he said apologetically. "I'm afraid I can't help you with writing." Then, in an almost reverent undertone: "Humans. Such power!"

Julie wondered why Al kept talking about "humans" and "power." She definitely didn't have any power, but she wished she did. Then she could return home.

"Maybe I'll write about dragons," she mused, toying with one bridle strap. Just then Al stumbled, and the strap fell out of her hand. It hung limply from the halter, out of her reach.

"Dragons? What are they?" Al stopped and grabbed the end of the strap in his teeth, reaching his head back to give it to her.

"Sort of . . . big lizards with wings and teeth," she answered, clutching the strap tightly.

"Ah, I see." Al's tone told her that he didn't see, but the gebra was too polite to inquire further.

They traveled for several hours, easily, and after the novelty of riding a gebra faded, Julie found that she was starting to get bored and a little tired.

"So, Al," she said, "how long have you lived in the gebra herd?"

"All my life," replied Al, apparently not tired in the least. "I was born into the herd, as all gebras are." Al told her about the Main Gebra, and his mother, and the Teacher Gebra, whose hindquarters were decorated in the pattern of a black-and-white composition notebook.

When it got dark they camped out on the open plain, Julie cuddled against the gebra's side as he lay in the grass. Julie was afraid of bugs crawling over her in her sleep, but Al assured her that the warm, red blanket she was curled up in—he had pulled it from one of the saddlebags—was made of insect-repellent material. "After all," he said, chuckling, "you creatures without tails need something to keep the insects away."

$$\{3[3+(2\times6)]\}+[4(13-6)]=$$

Julie awoke as the first rays of the sun touched her face. She lay in the deep green grass, breathing in the dry, vegetable smell of it. Al was a few feet away from her, his legs tucked under and his tail straight out. His head was up and he was sniffing the fresh morning air.

"Jubilant morning," he said, glancing her way, as if that were the usual thing to say in the morning. Perhaps it was, among the gebras.

"Good morning, Al," returned Julie, rolling onto her back. As she stood up, she realized that she was stiff and sore. "Ow!" she exclaimed, flexing her arms and legs.

"It appears that you are not used to riding gebras," Al observed. "Fortunately, I feel fine." He shifted his ears to catch the sounds from all directions.

Julie took a few stiff steps toward the gebra, then stood uncertainly beside him. "What's for breakfast?" she asked, remembering suddenly—with help from her growling stomach—that she hadn't eaten any dinner the night before.

"Grass, of course," answered Al.

Julie grimaced. "I eat people food."

"Ah, then you'll most likely be wanting the food packed in the saddlebags." Al stood up awkwardly and reached back with his teeth to unfasten one of the saddlebags attached to his hindquarters, chuckling softly.

"There's food in there?" Julie peered into the saddlebag, but all she saw was a small sack filled with little white cubes. "I don't see any food in here." She took out the small bag. "Please don't tell me that this is what you mean by 'food.'"

"Of course it is." The gebra seemed genuinely surprised.

Julie grimaced again as she folded the blanket and put it into the saddlebag. It seemed she would be having sugar cubes for breakfast.

"You just put water on them," Al continued.

That explained it, Julie thought. Maybe they would expand so she could eat them in more than one bite. She followed Al to a nearby stream, set two of the cubes on the ground, scooped up a handful of water, and poured it onto the cubes. Then again, she mused, maybe they would dissolve and then she would have nothing to eat.

As the cubes absorbed the water, they began to expand and change color. Soon there was a neat pile of eight red apples sitting on the gravel beside the stream.

"Apples!" exclaimed Julie, astonished. "Two cubes make eight apples?"

"Of course," Al stated. "Haven't you ever seen cubed food before?"

"Cubed food?" Julie groaned. She should have known! In a land of math, cubed food made sense. She knew about cubed numbers—where you multiply a number by itself, then again—but she had never even imagined cubed food. Two cubes times two made four, times two made eight, which explained the pile of apples—sort of.

"Cubed food is made by a complicated mathematical process," Al told her as she bit into one of the apples. It was delicious.

"It's not that complicated," Julie contradicted. "I know how to cube numbers."

"Cubing numbers is easy. Food, no." Al sniffed at a patch of grass, then took an experimental bite.

"I'm sure it's the same process," said Julie uncertainly. "You just kind of . . . multiply an apple by two more apples."

Al looked up at her in astonishment. "That's amazing!" he exclaimed. "I never thought of it like that!"

Julie eyed the apples, wondering how in the world one could actually multiply an apple.

"You truly are a Human," said Al solemnly.

Julie took another bite of apple. Would adding more water cause it to multiply again? She decided not to find out.

After they had relaxed and munched for half an hour, Julie climbed onto the gebra's back and they took off across the grassland again. Within an hour, a dark forest-line came into view ahead, looking almost like a big, green cloud hovering above the field until they got closer and Julie could make out the brown tree-trunks.

"What is that place?" she asked.

"The Elemental Forest," replied Al. "That's where the Periodics live."

"Good," remarked Julie. They were almost there! Riding Al was fun, but she was getting very tired after two days of sitting on his back. She hadn't realized how strenuous an adventure could be.

They went into the dark forest. Julie's legs brushed past low branches, and she could hear the muted hum of insects in the foliage far above. The gebra followed a narrow path and soon came to a small glade in the woods which was covered with grass and dotted with tiny yellow and blue flowers. Here he stopped, took a deep breath, and bellowed, "LITHIUM!!"

Julie waited, wondering what would happen next. Not long afterward there was a flicker to the right, and a small, silvery-white horse entered the glade.

"Hello, Al!" he greeted them, in a jovial male's voice. "Who's your companion?" He eyed Julie with mild suspicion.

"Julie, this is Lithium," Al said politely. "Lithium, Julie. She's a Human," he added in a respectful undertone.

"A Human!" The small horse's ears went forward, expressing his surprise.

Julie paused, then carefully dismounted. "Hi, Lithium," she said in a friendly tone. Oh, his coat looked so soft! She was used to Al's fuzzy hide, but this one was different. He was a little smaller than Al, which was small in horse terms anyway, and built lighter than Al was. His coat had a metallic glow, and he seemed young and strong. A bold "Li" shone on his left shoulder in black. It shimmered occasionally as the light from the sun, which was now high in the sky, sparkled off the silvery fur underneath it.

Lithium let Julie get quite close to him, his clear blue eyes tracking her progress with mild interest, but he shied away from her touch. His eyes lit up with mischief. She frowned and tried to touch him again, and he dodged away once more. After that Julie gave up and didn't pursue him further. Lithium seemed faintly disappointed.

"We're hoping you can help us find a way for Julie to return home," said Al.

"Oh, yes," Julie agreed, remembering her mission with a jolt.

"Fine," said Lithium, his eyes still faintly amused. "Let me call my group-mates. It'll be a good thing to discuss in the Council tonight."

"Group-mates?" asked Julie. She turned around to face Al, as if he might have the answer to her question. Meanwhile Lithium came up behind her. His mouth closed on the back of her shirt. Julie jumped in surprise, but Lithium didn't mean her any harm. He carefully picked her up by her shirt and put her on Al's back. "We are Group IA, the Alkali Metals," he explained.

Together they trotted deeper into the woods, Lithium making strange noises in his throat. At first Julie thought he was trying to whistle and gargle at the same time, but she soon realized that the little horse was calling his group-mates. All at once, six other horses like Lithium appeared, trotting along beside them.

"Hey, it's a Human!" cried one of the new horses, and Julie was suddenly being sniffed all over and poked at with soft noses.

"Careful," Al instructed. "Don't push her off." The tassels of his long tail brushed across her back. After a few moments, they stopped in another glade, and Julie finally had a chance to look closely at the Periodics of Group IA.

The first little horse to her left was almost invisible, the merest silvery flicker. Julie could actually see through it to the trees and bushes that surrounded them. A bright black "H" showed clearly on its side, the only easily visible marking. "Hydrogen!" Julie exclaimed, recognizing the chemical symbol. Those boring hours in science class had finally paid off!

"Hello," answered Hydrogen in a female voice. Suddenly the little horse phased in to visibility, becoming milky-white. She was so light that she hardly seemed to touch the ground as she hovered on the edge of the glade. She was even smaller than Lithium, more like a pony than a true horse.

Julie turned to her right. She spied a dark "Cs" on a silvery-white hide and recognized the symbol for Cesium. Cesium looked more solid than Lithium and was much taller. Although he was built heavier, he still was light on his feet like the rest of them. Julie glanced around at the others. They all appeared especially alert and watchful. *Because of me?* wondered Julie.

"Cesium," she called softly, and Cesium approached her. Al swung his head around to watch Cesium's progress.

"Hello," Cesium said in a soft voice, nuzzling Julie's hand as she set it carefully on his long nose.

"You're nice," she told him. "Lithium wasn't. He wouldn't let me touch him." She pouted theatrically, glancing reproachfully in the diminutive horse's way. She hoped he felt guilty!

"Well, you really should be careful touching anyone in Group IA," Cesium warned her. "Several of us can set things on fire if we come in contact with water, which can be found on your skin. Usually Periodics only react with other Periodics, but there's always a chance. Besides," he continued, "Lithium's just shy. I used to be, but lately I've lost some of my rareness around people." Cesium winked humorously, and Julie heard Hydrogen giggle behind her. She wondered what was so funny.

"Because of the Human scientists," Hydrogen explained when Julie shot a puzzled look at her. "They've started using Cesium more in their laboratories. His elemental form, that is. So he's not as rare as he used to be." Julie assumed that Cesium's "elemental form" was the actual element called "cesium" that people in the Human world—her world—extracted from rocks, or wherever elements came from.

Julie caught a flicker of movement out of the corner of her eye and turned to catch a glimpse of another Periodic hiding in the forest. This one dwarfed all the others, a huge Clydesdale of a Periodic. Julie gaped. "Who is that?" she whispered.

"Francium," replied Hydrogen. "Speaking of rare elements, come on out, Francey."

Francium eyed Julie from his safe place among the trees, then took a few hesitant steps into the glade. A black "Fr" shone on his side, and to Julie's amazement he seemed to ripple as he walked.

"I don't think the Human scientists have been able to isolate a pure sample of Francium yet," Hydrogen remarked.

Julie nudged Al, who obligingly lay down so she could climb off his back. She took a few slow steps toward Francium, then a few more. How intriguing he was! Francium watched her carefully but didn't flinch when Julie put out a hand to touch his side. To Julie's disbelief, the skin gave way beneath her hand, and she could push several inches with little resistance. She withdrew her hand and gazed up Francium. He didn't show any sign of pain and was standing there very patiently, so she pushed on him again.

"My natural state is a liquid," Francium softly explained. His deep voice came to Julie almost as a whisper in her mind. "I can be a solid if that's more comfortable to you." This time when Julie pushed on his side, it did not give.

"It should be a while before the others get here," said Lithium, coming up behind her. He was so close she could almost—almost!—touch him. *Next time,* she vowed.

"What others?" she asked.

"The other Periodics," explained Lithium. He looked at her warily, and Julie wondered whether he was keeping his distance because she was a human.

"Until then," said Al, turning from his conversation with another Periodic, "you can rest and bathe. There's a pool in the next glade. Kalium will watch over you."

Julie looked at the Periodic Al had been talking to, who was labeled "Na." She knew that was the symbol for Sodium. He was larger than Hydrogen and Lithium, but much smaller than Francium—or Cesium, for that matter. In fact, he was about Al's height, only a little smaller. There was another, larger Periodic behind Sodium, with an "Rb" on its side, but Julie did not know what that symbol meant.

She sighed. She didn't relish the idea of bathing in a muddy pool in the middle of a forest, particularly in front of a bunch of males, even if they were horses. However, she did feel dirty and tired from the trip, so . . . .

Another horse, soft and silvery-white like Lithium and Cesium, came up beside her and motioned with its nose for her to get on. Although lighter and smaller than Cesium, it was heavier and larger than Lithium. It had a dark "K" on its side, which shone more brightly silver than the hides of the other horses.

Lithium came up behind her again, and Julie asked him, "Who's that beside Sodium?"

"That's Rubidium," said Lithium. "He's also kind of shy." He gave her a boost up with his mouth as before, and Julie suddenly found herself trotting across the glade on the strong, shiny back of "K."

3

The Council in the Clearing

"ARE YOU KALIUM?" JULIE ASKED.

The horse she was riding laughed in a deep voice. "No, Kalium's my Isotope-sister. I'm Potassium."

"Oh," said Julie. "I didn't know elements had brothers and sisters!"

"They have Isotopes," said Potassium.

"What is an isotope?" inquired Julie.

Potassium trotted on smoothly for a moment in silence, then answered, "You know what an atom is, right?"

"Of course," replied Julie. She had learned that in the fourth grade. "The smallest part of anything. The building-block of all matter, too tiny to see with an ordinary microscope." She sighed, wondering if her former science teacher was still making atomic theory seem as boring as it had been when she was learning it.

"Right," stated Potassium. "The atom consists of a cloud of negatively-charged electrons circling around a nucleus. The nucleus is made up of many bits, but the two major ones are protons and neutrons. Protons are positively-charged, but neutrons are electrically neutral. Get it? Neutrons—neutral."

"Got it," Julie replied.

"Well, atoms make up the elements, too," Potassium continued. "In fact, the different kinds of atoms are named after the elements—or is it the other way around? Anyway, all of the atoms in a pure sample of an element are the same—that element's specific kind of atom. Same number of protons, same number of electrons in every atom. Everything besides elements—you know, molecules, compounds, mixtures, and so on—well, they are made of a lot of different kinds of atoms stuck together in all sorts of arrangements, but pure elements are all one kind of atom. Right. Anyway, every atom in an element has the same number of protons in the nucleus as electrons circling around it, but the number of neutrons differs. Am I making sense?"

"They have the same amount of electrons and protons, but not neutrons?" Julie felt like she was back in physical science class. Her head was spinning, but somehow she could comprehend what Potassium was telling her.

"Right . . . basically. For instance, my friend Tin has 50 electrons, 50 protons, and 68 neutrons. His nine Isotope-brothers and sisters have anywhere from 62 to 74 neutrons, but they all have 50 electrons and 50 protons."

They were in the thick forest now, but Julie could see brighter green ahead—a glade.

"How many neutrons do you have, Potassium?"

"Twenty."

They arrived at the glade, and Potassium motioned for her to get off by pointing his nose at her and jerking it toward the ground. Julie jumped to the thick grass and looked around. Near the far end of the small meadow was a clear pool fed by a large stream. Beside the pool waited a horse almost identical in appearance to Potassium, complete with a "K" on its side, except that its mane was longer and its eyes were gray instead of Potassium's blue.

"Hello," called Julie. "Are you Kalium?"

"I certainly am," replied the horse. To Julie's relief, it had a female voice. She wouldn't have to bathe in front of a male.

"Go on back to the group, Potassium," Kalium instructed. "I'll take over from here."

After Potassium left, Julie enjoyed a wonderful bath in the clear pool. She discovered that the shallow water around the edges was warm from the sun. Kalium helped her bathe and dry off, and then Julie stretched out on the grass against Kalium's side, beneath a blanket. The sun beat down on her face, the insects hummed high in the tree-tops, and the soft lapping of the water in the pool soon made her very drowsy. Before she knew it, Julie was asleep.

$$\{3[3+(2\times 6)]\}+[4(13-6)]=$$

When she awoke, the sun was gone and Kalium was standing over her.

"Good evening," said Kalium gently as Julie sat up. Then she pursed her equine lips in concern. "You shouldn't have gone to sleep with your hair wet, dear. Look at it!" Shaking her head ruefully, Kalium walked over to a small wooden chest sitting in the grass beside the pool. She opened the chest with her mouth, withdrew a brush, and brought that and Julie's clothes over to her. The latter had been drying on a rock in the sun. They had been scrubbed almost as thoroughly as Julie herself.

"Get dressed and I'll brush your hair," Kalium declared, dropping Julie's clothes at her feet.

They were still a little damp, but Julie put them on anyway. Then she sat still and let Kalium brush her hair. The brush really wasn't made for human hair, and it pulled horribly.

"What time is it?" Julie asked. Despite the absence of the sun, she could see quite clearly, and the trees blocked the moon (if there was a moon). She looked around for the source of the light.

"It's around eight o'clock," responded Kalium, returning the brush to the wooden chest.

Julie spotted several large lamps hanging high in the trees, fashioned from colored paper. They were the reason the forest was light, even at night.

"Up, up!" cried Kalium from behind her. "Let's go!"

As they traveled through the lamplit forest, Julie wondered about the Periodic Council, the group she and Al were on their way to meet. The Main Gebra had indicated that they might be able to help her return home. She hoped so. Her parents must be worried by now.

"The Council is already in session," Kalium told her, breaking into her thoughts as if she could read them. They pulled up at the edge of a huge clearing, and Julie looked around. Numerous lamps hung from the trees, revealing a giant herd of horses gathered around a wooden platform in the center of the glade. Julie gasped. There were more horses here than she had ever seen in her life—at least a hundred. They came in almost every color and size she could imagine, although most were shades of gray or silver.

"Are these all the horses there are?" she breathed, enthralled.

"Horses?" inquired Kalium, tilting back her ears. At first Julie thought she had taken offense, but Kalium's tone was merely curious as she went on. "Ah, yes. Al told me. You like to call us by that strange name, 'horses.' The answer to your question is no. These are only the Periodics. The Isotopes usually do not attend Council meetings."

"What's the difference between Periodics and Isotopes?"

"Well, each Periodic represents one element, including all of that element's Isotopes," Kalium explained.

"What do you mean?" Kalium had Julie's attention now—at least, most of it. Julie still looked over at the herd in admiration from time to time.

"My brother Potassium is a Periodic," explained Kalium. "He is the representative of all of our Isotope-brothers and sisters, who are called the Potassium Isotopes. He is the average of all our atomic mass numbers."

"What's an atomic mass number?"

"The atomic mass number is what you get when you add the protons of an element's atom to its neutrons. For instance, all of my atoms have 19 protons and 20 neutrons, so my atomic mass number is approximately 39. Each Potassium Isotope has a different atomic mass number, because each has a different number of neutrons. Understand? I heard you and Potassium talking about Isotopes on the way over."

Julie wondered just how sharp Kalium's hearing must be. "I guess I understand," she said, thinking hard. "So the Potassium I met is the . . . the average of you all? You add up all the Isotopes' atomic mass numbers, then divide by the number of Isotopes, and that gives the average, which is Potassium's atomic mass number?"

"Right."

"So his atomic mass number is exactly in the middle of all his Isotopes' numbers? And that's why he's a Periodic?"

"Exactly!" Kalium seemed genuinely pleased. "He's our representative. And I'm an Isotope—or, if you want to get technical, I'm an exception to the whole system. But that's another story." Kalium arched her ears forward and Julie glanced at the sea of horses. She noticed Al and Lithium standing on the platform in the middle, deep in conversation, but she couldn't hear what they were saying.

Julie wondered when they were going to enter the sea of horses, but she didn't inquire. Kalium would tell her when it was time. She would be patient until then.

"So, how many horses—er, Periodics—are there?"

"About a hundred and twenty."

"What? But I thought there were only a hundred and four elements!"

Kalium glanced back at her. "Oh! I'm sorry. That's right. The Human world has only discovered a hundred and nine, and they can only agree on a hundred and three. But you didn't really think that was all that existed, did you?"

"No, I guess not," said Julie doubtfully. "So there's actually a hundred and twenty?"

Kalium seemed to consider, her head slightly tilted. "Give or take some functionary Isotopes, yes. The Council tends to be a big affair."

"But what's the Council for?"

"The Council is where the Periodics gather to address issues needing attention. For example, there is the matter of Tungsten and the Wolframs—but that doesn't concern you. It is also where others may come to seek help. The Periodics are very wise. Maybe one of them will know a way for you to return home."

How did Kalium know about her problem? Julie shrugged off the annoying question. She was nervous now, her mind flitting around, generating needless questions. Probably Potassium had told Kalium when she was asleep.

"When are we going in?" she asked, forgetting her prior resolution to be patient.

"As soon as they call for us," replied Kalium. "Just relax. You're not on trial." Kalium flicked her tail gently, touching Julie's arm, and shifted her weight. Julie wondered if 107 pounds of human was too much for the little horse to carry. After all, Kalium was rather small for a Periodic—or an Isotope, she corrected herself quickly.

"I remember when I was a Periodic," Kalium went on dreamily.

"You were a Periodic?" Julie was stunned. How could that be?

"Oh, yes. A long time ago. Back then, the Potassium Isotopes were called Kalium Isotopes." Julie could imagine a reminiscent smile on Kalium's face as she recounted her history. "Ferrum, Aurum, Argentum, and Hydrargyrum, too," added Kalium, "as well as others. We were all Periodics. Now we're names of the past."

She shifted her weight again. "Our names come from Latin, mostly, and I think they're still used in some countries today. But our contemporaries, the modern Periodics who have replaced us, have taken over all our duties, even those for which the old names are still used." She paused thoughtfully before going on. "It really started with the American scientists, I suppose. Or the English. For whatever reason, they decided to call my Isotopes 'Potassium,' but they kept the 'K' from 'Kalium' for the elemental symbol. It's the same with Tin, whose elemental symbol is 'Sn' for 'Stannum.'

"Anyway, finally almost everyone started calling us Potassium Isotopes and my name faded into the history books." Kalium sighed but didn't sound too sad. "So I retired and became an Isotope, although technically I'm not really an Isotope-sister of Potassium the Periodic. More like . . . a cousin, really. Or a parent. I get lots of rest, which is good for me, and occasionally I drop by the Human world to check on how my element's doing." Kalium chuckled, then perked her ears at the platform. "It's time. Here we go!"

Kalium took off, entering the clearing with a bound and bearing Julie briskly through the crowd of Periodics, which parted obligingly to let them pass. They climbed up onto the platform by way of a sturdy wooden ramp, and Kalium asked her to dismount. As she surveyed the crowd, Julie's heart gave a leap. She somehow made her way down to the floor, nearly tripping as her knees almost gave out, and stumbled over to Al, who nodded to her encouragingly and nuzzled her hair. She clenched her fingers in his soft fur and tried not to look at the creatures all around her.

"Attention, Periodics!" called Lithium, and the crowd below stirred and buzzed quietly. Lithium moved over to her and nudged her, perhaps sensing her overwhelming stage fright. *What am I doing here,* Julie asked herself, *in the middle of a strange forest, surrounded by horses representing the elements in the Periodic Table?* Julie tried to hide behind Al so they couldn't see her, but Lithium pushed her gently to the front of the platform.

Julie stood stiffly, with the brightly-colored lamplights overhead in the trees reflecting softly off her hair. Hundreds of mild equine eyes focused on her as she shivered, frozen in fear. Then Kalium, who was still on the platform, came up beside her and pressed her warm, furry hide against Julie's shaking body. Taking stock of the Council, she nuzzled Julie's hair like Al had and took a deep breath.

"Brothers and Sisters!" she called then, in an authoritative voice that bounced off the farthest trees. "You see before you a real Human."

Julie found herself recalling how Kalium had told her she had once been a Periodic. Now she believed it! With that commanding note in her voice, Julie could tell that Kalium was used to being obeyed. She reminded Julie vaguely of her school's vice-principal.

There was another stir in the crowd as the Periodics nodded and whispered among themselves. It seemed that humans caused a commotion wherever they went in this strange land. Julie sighed.

"There is power," stated one Periodic stoutly. "I see it." The others around him nodded.

"No," said Kalium. "She is young and lost. Her powers are unfocused."

"The Mathematician did not send her?" one asked in an incredulous voice.

"No. She is wandering, trying to find a way home."

"Only the Mathematician knows the way!" exclaimed one.

"Yes, yes!" several cried simultaneously. "Send her to the Mathematician! He'll know what to do!"

When Julie turned to look at Al in confusion, the gebra's eyes were wide in astonishment.

"The Mathematician!" he exclaimed. "I should have thought of that in the first place!"

"That's settled, then," Kalium said firmly. "Now, what other issues do we need to address?"

Julie sat at the back of the platform for the rest of the night while the Council met, but she didn't really listen. Her eyelids grew heavier and heavier as time went by. Drowsily she wondered if the Periodic, Lead, had done something to affect them.

The Mathematician is the ruler of this land, she remembered, half asleep. *Why, oh why, did I ever follow that Imaginary Number through the portal in my room? I must have been a fool . . . . I wonder if Mom and Dad have called the police yet, and if they're searching around my room for clues, messing with my teddy bears and toy horses . . . . If only they could see me now, surrounded by real horses—except they're not horses . . . .* Julie dozed.

"Wake up!" Kalium said, nudging her. "Watch this." Julie sat up, rubbing her eyes. Hydrogen and Oxygen, who was a light gas Periodic in Group VIA with a bright "O" emblazoned on her side, stood side-by-side and concentrated on a spot on the forest floor. As Julie watched, a large puddle formed.

"Dihydrogen oxide," said Hydrogen contentedly. "Plain old water. I like making it because I get to double up on old Oxygen. There are two hydrogen atoms for every oxygen atom in water." She laughed and glanced sidelong at Potassium.

"No, no," asserted Kalium, "I want to do it." Potassium looked mildly surprised, but that was nothing compared to what Julie felt when she observed what happened next. "Step back," ordered Kalium, and put one forehoof in the puddle. As Kalium gazed down at the water, Julie saw a small white lump begin to form in the center. Immediately there was a great explosion. Purple light exploded outward, sparks flying everywhere—including onto the dry tinder they had placed nearby. By the time the explosion had ended, there was a nice bonfire going.

"Wow!" cried Julie. "That's great!"

"Thank you," said Kalium humbly.

"I didn't know you exploded!" said Julie.

"I don't," Kalium explained, "but in water my element forms a strong base, lots of hydrogen gas, and enough heat to ignite the gas. That was the explosion."

Julie settled down in the fire's warm glow, listening to the others around her murmuring something about "Tungsten" and "Wolframs." In a matter of seconds, Lead had conquered her eyelids once again, and she was fast asleep.

4

The Orders of Operations

IN THE MORNING THEY WASTED NO TIME, BUT GATHERED UP A small group consisting of Al, Lithium, Julie, and Hydrogen, plus two mysterious others, and set off out of the Elemental Forest, with Julie comfortably seated on Al's back. They did not go back the way Al and Julie had come into the forest, nor did they go in the opposite direction, but traveled at an angle from it. Navigating a series of tangled paths through the forest, they soon emerged on a wide grassland which looked exactly like the one Julie and Al had passed over to get to the Forest.

Walking slightly behind Hydrogen and to either side of her like a double mirror-image were two lookalike horses. They were very shy and wouldn't let Julie near them. Hydrogen introduced them as Deuterium and Tritium. "They're my Isotope-brothers," she explained. "I have one more, Protium, but he's very busy. He's the most abundant of us all, in Human terms. Quite a lot to do."

Julie noticed that the symbols on the Isotopes' sides looked different from those on the Periodics. Instead of chemical symbols she recognized, the Isotopes had letter-number combinations in their fur. Tritium's was ${}^{3}_{1}H$; Deuterium's was ${}^{2}_{1}H$.

"What do those little numbers mean?" Julie asked Al.

"You'd better ask someone else," the gebra replied apologetically. "Science isn't my specialty."

"It's very simple," Hydrogen said, coming up beside Julie and Al. "They identify Tritium and Deuterium as Isotopes. The bottom number is the atomic number, which is the number of protons. The top number is the atomic mass number, which—"

"I already know what an atomic mass number is," Julie interrupted. "Kalium told me yesterday." She was surprised that she remembered Kalium's explanation so clearly. Maybe science wasn't as hard—or as dull—as she thought. Or maybe it was more fun to learn it from horses than humans.

They rode for several hours and stopped for lunch around noon.

"Exactly where are we going?" Julie inquired as she ate an uncubed sandwich and drank from a clear, cool stream.

"To the Mathematician's Castle," Lithium replied.

"Does all of the scenery look like this?" Julie indicated the flat, featureless plain around them. "If it does, this is going to be a really boring trip."

"Oh, no," Lithium assured her. "We'll be passing through all six Orders of Operations on our way to the Castle. Each one is different."

"The orders of operations?" Julie repeated with a sinking feeling.

"Yes," answered Lithium. "Parenthesis, Exponent, Multiplication, Division, Addition, and Subtraction."

"There are places named after the six operations?" asked Julie skeptically. This definitely didn't sound good. The order of operations had gotten her into this mess in the first place, just because she hadn't known which came first in solving an algebraic equation.

After lunch, Julie climbed up onto Al's back and they rode until sunset, when the entrance to a huge cave came into view.

"What's that?" demanded Julie suspiciously.

"That is the entrance to Parenthesis," Al replied.

"Oh, no!" Her suspicions were confirmed; this was going to be a terrible trip. She had no desire to enter a deep, dark cave.

"We'll wait until morning to go in," Hydrogen explained.

At least she had some time before they set off into that horrible yawning blackness. By nightfall, they had reached a patch of grassland near the front of the cave, and Julie ate dinner while Al and the others grazed. After dinner, she slept curled up between Al and Hydrogen, with Lithium in front of her and Deuterium and Tritium on either side of them.

$$\{3^{[3+(2\times6)]}\}+[4(13-6)]=$$

In the morning they all ate in their respective fashions. Then Julie got up onto Al's fuzzy back, still with many misgivings.

"It's okay," soothed Hydrogen, noting her expression. "It's perfectly safe."

"Unless you're afraid of tight places," put in Deuterium softly.

"Claustrophobic," elaborated Tritium. As they gradually got used to her, Julie noted, they were losing some of their shyness, although Deuterium seemed naturally bolder than Tritium.

"Well, let's not just stand out here," said Lithium. "Let's go on in." Together they followed a worn path into the large cave entrance.

At first Julie was frightened, but the caves were well-lit with fluorescent moss and lichen, and there were no bats, bears, or huge spider webs blocking the passage.

"See, it's not so bad," said Al cheerfully. "This is a much-traveled region. There's nothing in it that would attack us, especially nothing that would dare to attack a Human."

"Nothing," agreed Julie faintly, eyeing the damp ceiling and walls. Nothing, except extra-curly hair and maybe a cold. She shivered uncomfortably, and Hydrogen brought the red blanket out of Al's saddlebags and draped it over her shoulders. The blanket was warm and soft, and so was Al's hide. Julie felt her reservations and fears slowly draining away. She was safe here, among friends.

"You see, Julie," explained Lithium, in front of her, "Parenthesis is a network of circular caves, each containing a smaller cave inside. They are connected by doors which open only when you solve the problem inside each one."

"Problem?" asked Julie, alarmed.

"Oh, it's usually not anything hard," Lithium confided. "Fit the right-shaped key into the hole, or take blocks of different shapes and separate them into bowls. It's never anything any one of us couldn't do. The problems are meant to keep creatures of low intelligence from crossing into Higher Mathematics."

"Into what?"

"Higher Mathematics," explained Lithium. "The inner part of the country. Most of the larger cities and buildings are there. We're right on the edge."

"What creatures of low intelligence?" Julie wanted to know. Did that by any chance include her?

"Oh, destructive monsters and such," said Al. "Don't worry. They're all but wiped out today."

"MONSTERS?!!!"

"Calm down, Julie. There are none in here." Al twisted his neck around to give her a square look.

"Ah, here we are!" exclaimed Lithium suddenly.

"Here we are where?" inquired Julie, peering around Al's neck to see what Lithium was talking about.

"We're out of the tunnel leading to the caves, and into the caves themselves."

"The caves themselves?" gulped Julie. She pulled her blanket tight around her.

"Yes. Come on."

They walked up a broad stairway, with steps far enough apart to allow for equine bodies, into a small, round chamber. By the light of the lichen, Julie could see a short, squat pedestal made of the dark gray rock of the cave itself. She also noticed two doors of slightly lighter-colored rock, one on either side of the cave.

"What is this place?" Julie asked.

"The innermost cave, Julie. This is Cave 1:1." Lithium led the procession to the pedestal.

"And what is this?" sighed Julie, looking at the pedestal. By now she was used to surprises—or so she thought.

"The problem. See? Nothing difficult." Lithium stepped up to the pedestal, gave a snort, and pushed a large round section in its center labeled "ENTRANCE" with his hoof.

The doors slid slowly sideways, exposing the chambers behind them.

"That was the problem?" Julie asked. "Pushing the word 'entrance' with your hoof?"

"Yes," replied Al.

"It certainly didn't seem very difficult."

"They get slightly harder."

"Do you mean to tell me that some dumb monster couldn't figure that out by himself?"

"Perhaps he could solve that one. But they do get harder."

"Which door do we go through?" Julie wanted to know.

"The one in the direction we're going," Lithium answered, nodding at it. "Toward Higher Mathematics. If we were returning from Higher Mathematics to Science, we would take the other door. I've been here before, and I know the way. We won't get lost."

They walked through the door into a drafty chamber. In the dim light, Julie could see that the wall behind her curved backward to form the sides of the chamber they had just exited. She looked forward and found that instead of forming a small chamber, the side walls here were farther away to either side, and they also curved behind them. A long way ahead, Julie sighted the dim glimmer of another curving wall.

"This is Cave 1:2," remarked Hydrogen. She pointed with her nose at a small sign engraved in the wall, which said the same.

They approached the next pedestal, about halfway across the cave floor, which looked almost exactly like the first, except that this one had four buttons. Each button had a mishmash of letters written on it, but only one spelled out "ENTRANCE." This was the one Lithium pushed, and a door across the cave opened promptly.

They hurried out of Cave 1:2 and entered Cave 1:3, which was like Cave 1:2, only bigger. This time Julie could not see any side walls at all, and the far wall seemed very far away indeed. She shivered, and Hydrogen nuzzled her gently.

"It's a little drafty," Hydrogen commented, "but there's no danger here."

"Sure," agreed Julie noncommittally.

This time the problem was to spell out the word "entrance" with a given number of tiles, each with a letter written on it.

"See? Could a monster do this?" asked Al. Julie didn't reply.

This time when the problem was solved, instead of a door opening into another, larger cave, a stairway appeared, leading down. They descended the stairway and entered a tunnel that stretched both ways, behind and before them.

"Which way?" asked Julie.

"The way we're going," replied Lithium calmly.

The tunnel dead-ended at another stairway, leading up, and they ascended obediently.

Julie found herself in another small chamber, like the first they had entered. "What is this?" she demanded. "Aren't we supposed to be in a large cave?"

"You always start from the innermost Parenthesis," Al reminded her.

Oh, right, Julie remembered. *You start at the innermost, do all the math there, and work outward. At least, that's what you were supposed to do with a math problem. But this was real.*

"This is Cave 2:1," Lithium commented, approaching the pedestal.

Caves 2:1, 2:2, and 2:3 were exactly like Caves 1:1, 1:2, and 1:3, except that their problems were different. In the first cave, it was a matter of putting a key made of rock into a hole in the pedestal. In the second, they had to put a rock key into the one hole out of four that was labeled "ENTRANCE." In the third, they had to choose the key that was labeled correctly and put it in the correct hole.

They descended another stairway into a tunnel, followed the tunnel to a stairway leading up, and entered caves 3:1, 3:2, and 3:3. Like the previous caves, they were the same, except for their problems. When they followed the tunnel leading away from Cave 3:3, they found themselves outside.

"Hooray!" cried Julie impulsively. "We made it!"

"We certainly did," stated Al.

"Was there any doubt?" inquired Deuterium nervously.

"Of course not, Deu," Hydrogen reassured him.

It was late afternoon, and they feasted on grass and sandwiches.

"What do you think, Lithium?" Al asked the silvery Periodic after their meal. "Do we go on?"

"I dunno, Al," returned Lithium, eyeing the sun. "It's pretty late. A misstep in the dark, in the middle of Exponent, and it's over."

That sounded pretty morbid to Julie, so she immediately wanted to know all about this next hurdle. "What is Exponent?" she asked, interrupting their debate.

"Exponent is a group of high towers made of rock," explained Lithium, "each representing one of the Powers of Mathematics."

"The what?"

"The different functions and operations of Mathematics. The Powers of the land. In the center of each is a keyhole, and if you have the proper key you can turn that Power off or on."

"Oh," said Julie. "But how do we get from tower to tower?"

"We jump," replied Lithium. "It's never a great leap, but I wouldn't want to make it in the dark."

Julie shivered, appreciating his concern. "Then we'd better wait until tomorrow," she said.

"Yes, we'd better. We could use some rest, anyway."

The others agreed, and they all settled down for the remainder of the day to frolic in the grass and snooze.

$$\{3^{[3+(2\times 6)]}\}+[4(13-6)]=$$

When Julie awoke, there was a glimmer of light in the east.

"I wonder what time it is?" she grumbled quietly to herself.

"It's time to watch the sunrise," Lithium answered.

"Oh! Hello, Lithium. I didn't know you were up." Julie sat up and pulled at her tangled hair.

Lithium snorted. "It's my watch."

"Your watch?"

"Yes. Al, Tritium, and I kept watch this night, rotating turns."

"Oh. Tomorrow night I guess I'll keep watch." Julie didn't exactly relish the idea, but she felt guilty about getting a full night's sleep.

"Yes. You and Hydrogen and Deuterium. Now, let us go see the sunrise."

Julie stood stiffly and followed the Periodic to the edge of a huge, strange area. In the dim predawn light she could see a flat, rocky surface, broken regularly by deep, dark cracks. As the light improved she saw that the cracks ran and split and re-connected to form large, roughly circular islands of rock, each only a few feet apart from its neighbor. This went on as far as the eye could see, in every direction except behind them, where the caves of Parenthesis were.

"This is Exponent?"

"Indeed." Lithium seemed very somber at the moment, so Julie became quiet and watched the horizon to the east, which was defined only by more islands of rock, stretching on and on.

Slowly the light increased, and the sky lightened significantly from a midnight blue to a light pink, then yellow, then light blue and red, all mixed together. Then, slowly, the sun lifted itself over the rocks, as red as fire.

Julie's mind drifted as she watched the beautiful spectacle. She began to think about the sun. It wasn't made of fire, it was made of plasma, which was electrically charged stuff made of the nuclei of atoms—they had lost all of their electrons, and were floating around randomly.

"Plasma," she murmured very quietly. Plasma sounded like the name of a beautiful but fierce lady. Maybe it had been named after a Greek goddess.

"Plasma?" inquired Lithium. "That's one of the States of Matter."

"Yes," agreed Julie. She had learned about the four states of matter in science. Every object was in one of the states: rocks were solid, water was liquid, air was gas. And stars were plasma.

The sun had hauled itself up over the rocks and had begun to look orange rather than red. Soon it would be its normal yellow hue. Then Julie's mind jumped. The states of matter! Knowing this world, they could be real places!

"Where are the States of Matter, Lithium?" she asked.

"Over to the northwest, past Elemental Forest."

So they *were* real! "All four states are represented? Solid, liquid, gas, and plasma?"

"Oh, yes. I've been to the Solid State, the Liquid State, and the Gaseous State."

"Haven't you ever been to the Plasma State?"

Lithium seemed to choke. "The Plasma State! No one goes into the Plasma State! At least, no one who ever comes out to tell about it."

"Why not?"

"You just don't!"

"Strange things happen in the Plasma State," stated Hydrogen, coming up behind them.

"Like what, Hydrogen?"

"Fusion," answered Hydrogen, but she wouldn't say anything more, despite Julie's puzzled questions.

They awoke Al, Deuterium, and Tritium and ate breakfast, then stood surveying Exponent.

"Well, let's get going," sighed Lithium.

Julie looked across the cracked landscape in the full light of day, and saw that the cracks were much deeper than she had thought. Each island was a separate tower made of red-brown rock. They marched by the hundreds across a huge chasm. Also, the towers were not round, but hexagonal-shaped, like chambers in a honeycomb. In the center of each was a small, square hole, which had to be the keyhole Lithium had mentioned yesterday. If you had the right key, you could unlock the Powers of Mathematics. Julie wondered which Powers they might be. Addition? Subtraction? Maybe changing a decimal to a fraction?

"How long is it likely to take us?" inquired Al.

"A couple of hours," answered Lithium. "It's a strenuous effort. Julie, I'm afraid you'll have to walk today." He glanced at Al.

"Okay," replied Julie, not really pleased. "Is that because we have to jump from tower to tower?" She remembered that Lithium had said something about that the night before.

"Right," Al agreed, stepping onto the first one.

Lithium jumped across to the tower next to Al with a short hop, then jumped to the tower directly in front of him. "I'll lead," he remarked.

"That's fine," acceded Al. He looked rather nervous.

Julie glanced down as she stepped onto the first tower. She was feeling somewhat nervous herself. In fact, she felt rather sick. All she could see, for a long, long way down, was darkness where the sun couldn't reach. She picked up a pebble from the top of the first tower, crossed over to the edge, and dropped it into the next crevice. It fell down, down, into the increasing dimness, then disappeared into the dark. A long time afterward, she heard a faint *clunk* as it hit the bottom.

"A long way down, eh, Human?" commented Deuterium, touching her lightly from behind with his nose.

"Yes, indeed," she agreed, jumping quickly over to the next tower.

For the next few hours, they traveled single file, with Lithium leading, Al behind him, Julie behind Al, and Hydrogen, Deuterium, and Tritium bringing up the rear. Everyone was serious; nobody stopped to laugh or play. The spaces between the towers were too deep, and the risk of falling was too real.

5

Between Multiplication and Division

AROUND NOON THEY SAW, FAR AWAY, THE UNBROKEN LINE OF the other side of the chasm.

"We've almost made it!" Deuterium cried enthusiastically. Sweat dripped from his body, and he seemed to be panting. They were all in a similar state. It wasn't easy to propel an equine body forward in a series of short hops-and-walks for a long time, Julie realized. Or to propel a human body like that, she reflected, wiping sweat out of her eyes. It hadn't been this hot yesterday!

"It's farther than you think," Hydrogen told Deuterium gently. "It'll be awhile before we get there."

They decided to stop for lunch, and Al, the Periodics, and the Isotopes ate some hay they uncubed with water out of a canteen. Julie was surprised when her cube turned into a tuna salad. It tasted delicious. While screwing the top back on the canteen, Julie asked Al how he knew what a cube would turn into before he uncubed it, and Al said something about its smell. Julie sniffed one cube but couldn't smell anything.

After lunch and a short rest, they continued on. "We don't want to get stuck here at night," Al told her. "One of us could fall."

Julie glanced down and nodded. Then she looked at the distant grass on the far side of the chasm. It didn't seem so far away as to take them the rest of the day.

As she plodded on, she felt like they were in a huge ocean, and the end of the chasm, far ahead, was the shoreline.

"How long?" she panted, hopping across to the next island. *Number twelve thousand thirty-three? Fifteen billion? Sixty-two?* she asked herself.

"A few more hours," sighed Hydrogen from behind her.

Then it happened. Tritium, bringing up the very rear of the procession, misjudged the distance to the next island and his hind legs fell through.

"Help!" he called, holding onto the top of the tower as best he could with his front hooves.

They all ran back to him, and Julie, following Al's instructions, quickly ran a rope under Tritium's belly, behind the forelegs, and tied it tight. Then she ran the rope around him a second time, in front of his legs, and tied it again. Everyone grabbed hold of the rope and hauled valiantly, and Tritium was slowly dragged up onto the tower.

"Whew!" exclaimed Hydrogen, flicking the sweat from her sides with her tail.

"That was a job!" remarked Lithium, panting slightly.

"Thank you," gasped Tritium, working his way farther onto the island. The whites showed in his eyes, and his breath came in heavy gasps.

"You're okay, Tritium," Julie soothed him, flopping down beside him and wearily patting his neck. He had a few small cuts and scratches, but otherwise he was fine.

"Yes, thanks to you!" exclaimed Tritium. He nuzzled her exuberantly.

"It wasn't just me," Julie reminded him modestly. "I couldn't have pulled you up by myself."

"And the others couldn't have tied the rope around me fast enough," Tritium told her calmly, untying the knots with his teeth. Of course, because he had the rope in his mouth, it sounded more like "Anf de ofers coun'f haf died de wope awound me fasf enough," but Julie could understand well enough what he was saying.

Because of the accident, the others all agreed that they should rest for a couple of hours before continuing. Afterward, they finished the trip without further mishap.

It was dark as they came to the thick grass of the other side, and they ate quickly and went right to sleep.

$$\{3^{[3+(2\times 6)]}\}+[4(13-6)]=$$

In the morning, when she awoke, Julie saw nothing out of the ordinary. They were in a field, with grass and trees and small animals, stretching on and on. However, to the far left she saw a yellow glimmer, as of gold. She thought back through the order of operations—parenthesis, exponent, multiplication, division, addition, and subtraction—and concluded that they had reached Multiplication.

"Al," she called softly.

"Yes?" asked Al, coming awake with a start.

"We forgot to set a watch last night."

"So we did," mused Al. "Oh, well." He got up heavily, grimacing.

"Is this Multiplication?"

"Somewhere ahead is Multiplication," replied Al, peering about.

"But all I see is a field," Julie said.

"That's what Multiplication is," Al answered.

"A field?"

"You'll see."

When they had eaten and drunk their fill from a clear stream which trickled through the huge meadow, they prepared to leave.

Just as Julie was getting ready to climb up onto Al's back, Tritium nudged her from behind.

"I will carry you," he said, and as no one protested, Julie took the soft leather saddle off of Al, set it on the Isotope's back, and hopped on. She didn't even need Lithium to help her, Tritium was so small.

He was soft, too, she noticed, as they trotted slowly across the meadow, taking their time. They were following the stream for now. They traveled for about an hour, and Julie found herself getting bored. This was nothing compared to the adventure of yesterday! She tugged at a small hunk of Tritium's hair, and to her surprise it came out in her hand.

"Oh!" she exclaimed, looking at the fine white hairs that trailed between her fingers.

Tritium glanced back her way. "What is wrong?" he inquired.

"Some of your hair just came out."

Tritium nodded. "That's all right," he said. "Don't be worried. It's supposed to do that."

"Why?"

"Because I'm radioactive," he replied.

"Oh," said Julie, wondering what he meant. She tried to remember what she had learned in school about radioactive elements, and recalled that they were unstable and supposedly decayed, slowly losing parts of themselves over a span of time. Electrons and neutrons and protons just kind of came off. But Julie hadn't known that Tritium was one of them. She suddenly felt sorry for him.

"It's all right," said Tritium, as if sensing her distress. "Because I'm not actually a sample of my element, I don't really decay. I just lose hair. Don't worry about it." He shook his head in a reassuring way, flinging silky hair back at her.

"Okay, if you say so," responded Julie uncertainly. She turned her attention toward the scenery. It wasn't much different than what she had seen when she first traveled with Al toward Elemental Forest: a large, spreading meadow, green with grass and dotted here and there with trees. Even as Julie looked she spotted some geometrees, trigonometrees, and chemistrees.

The Periodics stopped in the shade of a chemistree to rest. Julie climbed down off of Tritium, lay down on her back beneath the spreading branches of the tall plant, and looked up, sighing in contentment. For being stranded in a strange world, this wasn't too bad.

Lithium was rubbing his side happily against the rough bark of the tree. "This is an Alkali Metal species," he stated, sticking his nose into the foliage. "I didn't know they grew so far into Mathematics!"

"Maybe someone transplanted it," suggested Hydrogen.

Julie stood up and examined the foliage. Each leaf had lobes on it like a maple leaf, except the leaves of this tree had eight lobes instead of five. There appeared to be fruit growing deep in the foliage. The fruit looked very much like something she had seen only in pictures.

"Are those atoms?" she demanded, pointing at the fruit, but Lithium shook his head.

"They only look like atoms," he confided. "If they were, I could make that lithium fruit"—he poked his nose at a tiny atom-like fruit—"react. I could make it bond with one of the other atoms, or do other things with it. Instead, I'll eat it." And he did.

"Is it good?" asked Julie dubiously.

"Yum, yum," commented Lithium enthusiastically between bites.

"I suspect it's only good to him," Hydrogen told her. "I wouldn't recommend that you eat it. It might make you sick."

Julie nodded and picked another fruit, larger than the one Lithium was cheerfully crunching away at. "What is this?" she inquired, turning it around in her hands. It had three rings encircling it, like a tiny Saturn. Julie looked closer and saw eleven tiny blue spheres in the rings. With a start, she realized that these were electrons, no longer moving but frozen. They were arranged in an orbit around a small nucleus which had eleven—she counted them—protons and eleven neutrons.

"A sodium fruit," replied Tritium, eyeing it. He reached down and took a small bite, breaking off several levels of electrons and part of the nucleus as well. "Hmm," he remarked then, munching on it thoughtfully. "Needs some salt."

All of the Periodics and Isotopes laughed for some reason, and Julie wondered why. Then she remembered that salt was made of sodium and chlorine, and joined in.

"Oh, that's funny!" she giggled. She handed the sodium to Tritium, who took it in his mouth and lay down in the warm grass to munch on it like a dog.

"This is an old tree," remarked Deuterium.

"How do you know?" inquired Julie, studying the slender trunk.

"Well, these atoms are Bohr models—that is, instead of being arranged in clouds, like in the newest Human theory, the electrons in these atoms are put into orbits, as if they're circling a planet. That's called the Bohr model of the atom, because a Human named Niels Bohr came up with it. It's been out of date for several years. That's probably why these trees are in Mathematics and not in Science. There, all the trees are up-to-date."

"Well, I guess it's time for us to be getting on," sighed Hydrogen.

The Periodics seemed loath to leave the tree, but they knew they had to be traveling on. They needed to be in Higher Mathematics by next week at the latest. There was another Council meeting after that.

Julie remounted Tritium, being careful not to touch the angry red scrapes along his flanks from his accident the day before, and they forged on across the wide meadow.

Around noon they stopped for lunch, and Julie asked Deuterium about the yellow glimmer up ahead and to the left of them that she had first seen that morning.

"That's Division," Deuterium told her. "Multiplication and Division run side-by-side, instead of one in front of the other. We're heading for the path that runs between them."

Julie looked down at her hands, wondering how long it would take to reach the path. She noticed that there was dirt under her nails. As she picked it out, it seemed to her that her fingernails were much longer than they had been yesterday. They usually didn't grow that fast.

The party set off again after lunch, and when it was almost dark they finally came to the path. It turned out to be a wide, clear road, paved with what appeared to be white concrete. On one side was Multiplication, with its lush vegetation, and on the other was Division, a huge desert with yellow sand and a few cacti. Since it was almost night, the desert animals were starting to come out. The animals in Multiplication were returning to their burrows.

"They're almost perfect opposites," Julie breathed.

"Wait until you see Addition and Subtraction," Tritium remarked, swiveling his ears back toward her.

"We'll stop here for the night," Lithium declared, veering off toward a small meadow in Multiplication where the grass looked especially thick and soft. "Nothing will bother us this near the path, so there's no need to post a watch."

"Better safe than sorry," warned Al, but Lithium brushed him away—quite literally, by swiping the gebra with the tip of his tail.

"We're safe," he insisted. *Safe from what?* Julie wondered.

$$\{3^{[3+(2\times 6)]}\}+[4(13-6)]=$$

Julie slept peacefully that night on a cushiony patch of grass, and when she awoke she looked at her fingernails again. They were definitely growing faster than they normally did. They were almost as long as the fake nails sold in stores that people glued onto their fingertips.

Julie sat up and looked around. Apparently Al's foreboding had been nothing, as everyone was here and safe. All of the others were still dozing.

"Hey, Tritium," she called softly, touching the small horse's neck.

"Eh, what?" asked Tritium, waking with a start.

"Good morning."

"Oh, yes. Good morning." One of the things Julie liked best about her companions was that they never complained when you woke them up. That was more than she could say about her little brother!

"How are you this morning?" she inquired.

"Oh, all right," yawned Tritium, still sleepy.

Julie gazed down his white furry hide. There was no sign of the scratches that had been there only yesterday.

"Your scratches are gone!" she exclaimed, surprised.

"Yes," replied Tritium. "That is the way of Multiplication and Division."

"I don't understand."

"In these regions, your cells divide and multiply faster, so any wounds you might have heal up about three times faster than they would normally."

"Oh, wow! So that's why my nails are growing so long." Julie thought that was neat.

She stood up and looked across the path toward the hot, dry desert on the other side. Then she looked down at the green grass around her feet.

"This place is weird," she remarked.

Tritium nodded, stood, and woke the others. Unlike Tritium, most of them did complain, ruining Julie's assumption.

As they started breakfast—Multiplication grass for the gebra, Periodics, and Isotopes, ordinary cubed food for Julie—she took stock of the tiny cubes she had left. There were only ten. Would that be enough? Julie went through the order of operations in her mind and concluded that she might have enough. As long as the Mathematician's Castle wasn't more than a day beyond the Orders.

"Al, how many days is it from here to the Mathematician's Castle?"

Al paused for thought, then replied, "About five days."

Uh-oh, thought Julie. *Ten cubes divided by five days equals two cubes a day.* Al apparently noticed her look, because he asked, "Is something wrong?"

"Not enough food for five days," replied Julie.

"Oh," said Al. "Well, we can collect some wild food. There are bound to be some plants around here that you can eat."

Julie nodded, though she was not at all convinced that she could eat any of the plants in this strange land. Would it all be like the atomic fruit of the chemistree?

Tritium rubbed against her, leaving some fine white hairs behind, and Julie climbed up on his back.

"Can I ask you something?" Julie wanted to know.

"Of course," Tritium replied.

"Earlier you said that cells divide and multiply faster around here."

Tritium nodded.

"So will my nails grow faster in Division, like they did in Multiplication?"

"Naturally," Lithium interrupted. "When cells divide, they multiply, and they multiply by dividing. It's all the same."

"Of course," said Al, coming up beside Tritium, "for the time we're on the path, we're immune to both effects."

"Oh," sighed Julie, disappointed. She had wanted to see how long her nails would grow during the day.

They made excellent time down the wide, paved path, though Julie's eyes hurt from the light glaring off the harsh white concrete. She tried to gaze into Division, but the sunlight reflecting off the sand was worse. Finally she looked into Multiplication, and that was easier. The scenery wasn't as monotonous as the desert, and it didn't reflect as much light as the path.

As they traveled, Julie thought about the way cells multiply and divide. She remembered that the process was called "mitosis," and it was pretty complicated. First, two round parts near the nucleus—"centrioles"—grew little fibers out in all directions, looking like tiny stars. At this stage they were called "asters." Julie thought of the word "astronaut" and wondered if the two words—aster, astronaut—came from the same root. *I'll have to check on that when I get back home . . .* if *I get back home,* she corrected herself.

Second, the asters separated and moved to opposite sides of the cell. Fibers grew between them, forming a bridge called a "spindle." The chromosomes were pulled by spindle fibers into a row along the middle of the cell. They split lengthwise in a way that made two copies of the same chromosome. At this point the centrioles—rather, the asters—split in two. As the spindle got longer, the chromosome pairs were separated on opposite sides of the cell by all the pulling fibers. When the spindle got long enough, it eventually pushed the two centrioles away from each other and they pulled apart, forming two new, whole cells. And somewhere in there, the chromosomes bundled back into a nucleus.

Julie sighed, glancing down at her fingernails. The more she thought about it, the more fascinated she became. Who had invented such a process? And how had they come up with it in the first place?

"What are you thinking about, Julie?" asked Al.

"Life," answered Julie. "And how it works."

"Oh," replied Al, nodding wisely. Then Julie heard him murmur very softly to himself, "Humans!"

6

The Path around Addition Mountain

THEY STOPPED FOR LUNCH, AND JULIE FOUND SOME RIPE berries growing on a low bush in Multiplication. Hydrogen confirmed that they were edible for humans, so she ate some. They were delicious.

"You're getting red juice all over your face," Deuterium told her, dubiously eyeing the part of her in question.

"That's all right," she said. "It's worth it." She picked another of the round little balls. The outside skin of the fruit was mostly red, touched with blue. But the inside was all red, very sweet and juicy.

What are these, anyway?" she wanted to know.

"Barometer berries," replied Al.

Julie rolled her eyes. Barometer berries! What a silly name! But somehow it made sense in this land. A barometer was a scientific instrument, used to measure pressure. Still, it had nothing to do with mathematics, only science.

"It looks like we're going to have a little rain," stated Deuterium, inspecting the berries on the bush. "They seem to indicate change."

"Bring some," Lithium instructed. "We can use them to tell how high we are in Addition."

"Good idea," proclaimed Hydrogen, nipping off some by the stems and placing them in one of Al's saddlebags.

"What's Addition?" asked Julie, as they continued on down the pathway.

"A mountain," replied Tritium from underneath her. "Quite tall. We have to go over it."

"Not precisely over it," Lithium explained quickly, as Julie looked nervous. "There's a path between it and Subtraction. But it isn't very straight. Sometimes it wanders up into Addition, and sometimes it goes down into Subtraction. We'll just follow it and be safe enough. But I told you to bring the berries so we can always tell just how high or low we are."

"How do you interpret the berries?" interrupted Tritium.

"Their color," replied Deuterium. "I'll show you, once we get to Addition."

"So Addition is a mountain," mused Julie. "What is Subtraction?"

"Guess," invited Al, nudging Lithium to be quiet just as the Periodic started to speak.

It didn't take Julie long. "A valley, right?"

"That's right," asserted Lithium. "Subtraction is as deep as Addition is tall."

"I can't wait to see it," said Julie. For one thing, she would be closer to the Mathematician's Castle, and for another, it sounded very interesting.

By the time it was dark they had come to the end of the path, and the grass swept over to engulf the left half of the scenery, where Division had dominated. Julie interpreted that to mean they had come to the end of Multiplication and Division, although the terrain all looked exactly like Multiplication. They camped in the middle of the wide, warm plain, and Julie found some fruits growing on a tree. They appeared to be normal oranges, but she didn't ask what they were—only whether they were safe to eat. Hydrogen assured her that they were.

"By mid-morning tomorrow we'll be at Addition," Al told

her, as she lay down to sleep beside him that night. "Then you'll see how tall it is."

"I've seen mountains before, Al," she informed him gently.

"In the Human world, yes. But you haven't seen Addition Mountain."

"Is it much different than any other mountain?"

"You'll see."

Julie relaxed with her arms underneath her head. For some reason, anything she ate here seemed to fill her up quickly, and after only a couple of oranges, a few berries, or one cube of cubed food, she was full.

Al pulled the blanket over her and Julie drifted off to sleep, dreaming of running around on a mountain made entirely of stacked oranges.

$$\{3^{[3+(2\times6)]}\}+[4(13-6)]=$$

In the morning the sky was overcast, and Julie was disappointed not to see the sunrise.

"Does it rain normally here?" she inquired. "I mean, does it rain just water? Not numbers or anything?"

"No," laughed Hydrogen. "Just ordinary H_2O. Oxygen and I are paid a small fee every year for the use of our elements here, for rain."

"Mathematics imports rain?" Julie found that very funny.

"No, but they have to pay for the elements they use every year," Hydrogen told her. "For instance, Lead used to get paid for the pencils they use in the castle—the Mathematician's, I mean. Now, of course, the pencils are graphite, so Carbon gets paid."

"Good old Pb," mused Lithium, saying the chemical symbol for lead. "He's a pretty nice guy. But now everyone's against him because there's something in the Human world called lead poisoning."

"I didn't know Lead could be poisoned," exclaimed Deuterium. "How can the Humans poison him?"

"They don't. He poisons Humans."

"Oh, no!" cried Deuterium. "That's awful!"

"Actually, a lot of children get lead poisoning," Julie said. "It's a serious problem. I know about it because I did a report for school."

"How does it happen?" Hydrogen wanted to know.

"Usually little kids eat old paint that chips or flakes off of walls or window sills or radiators. Paint used to have lead in it, and lead paint tastes sweet. Nobody knew for a long time that it was poisonous."

"Poor Humans," sighed Tritium.

"Poor Humans!" exclaimed Deuterium. "The Humans have more powers than we do, all put together!"

"What do you mean, we humans have powers?" asked Julie, puzzled. She was back to riding Al again, and she really meant the question for him. "I've heard talk about humans and our so-called powers ever since I got here. But I don't have any powers! If I did, I'd go home by myself and we wouldn't have to travel to the Mathematician's Castle."

"You just don't know how to use your powers," Al explained. "If you did, you *could* go home by yourself, and you wouldn't need the Mathematician's help."

"But what powers do we humans have?" Julie insisted.

"You can do math," said Al.

"And you understand science," added Lithium.

"But *I* can't do math! And *I* don't understand science!"

"Sure you do," said Hydrogen comfortingly. "What is two plus five?"

"Seven," replied Julie. "But everyone knows that. I know *you* know that."

"Yes, but it took us forever to learn it. How long did it take you?"

"About two weeks," said Julie, thinking back to the first grade.

"Well, it took me two months," Hydrogen told her.

"Why?"

"We're creatures of science. Math is not our specialty. Fortunately, math and science are closely related, so we can understand some. But think of language! We can't even begin to comprehend that!"

"Of course you can," said Julie gently. "Look down at your shoulder. That 'H' there, that's a letter. A letter is the beginning of language."

Hydrogen glanced down in surprise. "Why, so it is!" she exclaimed. "I never thought of it that way!"

"Can't you read?" asked Julie sympathetically.

"A little," responded Hydrogen vaguely. "Only a few words—enough to get me through Parenthesis. I never really tried to learn more than that."

"How about you, Al?"

"Same here," the gebra replied. "A few simple, necessary words. I can read any mathematical equation, but equations and sentences are two totally different things."

Julie pondered what she had just learned about her friends. Did they mean that if you were good at science and math, you couldn't be good at language? And if you were good at language, you couldn't be good at science and math? Julie knew plenty of humans who were good at all three. Sooner or later, she would be better at math and science than she was now. *I'm bound to be,* she told herself, *because I can't get much worse!*

The sun was well in the sky by this time, though still hidden behind the clouds, and Julie saw a spire rising up ahead of them. It appeared to be a few hundred feet tall. At first she thought it was a small tower, but soon she recognized it as a little mountain.

"Is that Addition?" she asked.

"The first few hundred feet of it," she was told.

As they traveled on, mile by mile, the spire grew much taller and thicker. Julie soon saw that it was a huge mountain, rising straight up out of the green plain.

"Isn't that curious," she mused out loud. "No foothills or anything."

"Foothills aren't necessary," Al told her. "You step directly onto the first part of addition when you're learning math, don't you? There is no way to prepare, except perhaps to learn the numbers themselves."

"So this plain, is it called the Numbers Plain?"

"No, I believe this part is called the Prime Plain. Over to the west it merges into the Composite Plain."

"Prime and composite numbers," murmured Julie. "So don't tell me—this plain can't be divided into smaller parts, but Composite Plain can be."

"How did you know that?" demanded Al.

"Just a lucky guess," said Julie, grinning. Everything around here had to do with mathematics! She amused herself by making up silly statements and questions. *Prime Plain is a Partial Plain, and Composite Plain is a Complete Plain, and together they are a Complete Pain! Or is it the other way around?* She laughed, almost falling off of Al's back. *Prime numbers make up composite numbers; do Prime Plains make up Composite Plains?*

"What is so funny?" asked Al, swiveling his dainty ears back at her.

"Oh, nothing," giggled Julie. "Just joking to myself." She gave a last, amused chuckle, then settled down.

By noon, they had almost reached the foot of the huge, rocky mountain. They stopped to rest but did not have lunch. "We can eat somewhere in Addition," stated Hydrogen.

Julie inspected the mountain. "How tall is it?" she asked.

"Nobody knows," Al told her. "Except maybe the Mathematician."

"Why should he know and not anyone else?"

Al looked puzzled. "Maybe someone else knows." He shook his head. "I don't know. All I know is that I don't know how tall it is, and no one else knows that I've ever met."

"How long should it take us to scale it?" inquired Tritium, gazing up with awe in his calm brown eyes.

"Haven't you ever seen Addition Mountain before, Trite?" Julie asked, reaching out with one hand to pat him in a friendly fashion, slightly above the "$^{3}_{1}$H" on his shoulder.

"Never," answered Tritium in a faraway voice. "It's so huge!"

"I sense the presence of my element," Lithium stated soberly.

"Well, it's probably all mixed up with the rock and other elements in the mountain," said Julie, tearing her eyes from the daunting spectacle and looking around. "Where's the path?" she asked.

"To answer your question, Tritium," put in Hydrogen, who was nibbling delicately at a patch of fur just over her "H," "we don't have to scale it, remember? Just go around it. That should take only a couple of days."

Lithium, looking eagerly for the path, had trotted ahead into the waist-high undergrowth and disappeared around a large, thick bush with deep green foliage.

"Here it is," he called from somewhere behind it.

The others followed, picking their way through the grasses, and sure enough, there was the broad path that led around the mountain. Only this time, instead of being paved in white concrete, the path was of red-brown dirt. Julie climbed onto Al's back, and he and the others trotted quickly along the path. They kept their eyes on the ground without looking up toward the menacing summit.

"This place is too high," murmured Deuterium to Tritium, who nodded in solemn agreement.

Soon they came to a deep, dark chasm which opened up terrifyingly to the left of the path. Across the chasm there was more open plain, but it was impossibly far away and unreachable.

"That is Subtraction," remarked Al, pointing his ears at the huge crevasse. He did not go near the edge, but stayed far back on the broad dirt path, which now ran between the two Orders of Operations.

Julie glanced quickly up at the peak, then down, down, into the chasm. What Lithium had told her seemed to be true: Subtraction was as deep as Addition was tall. The canyon to her left was so very deep that the bottom was lost in darkness. Julie felt a surge of vertigo, worse than any she had experienced while hopping rock-to-rock across Exponent. She tugged on Al's mane to keep him safely back from the edge, but he needed no guidance.

"Let's just get going," she said shakily. "This place is too high and too low for me!"

"I agree!" said Tritium and Deuterium, and Hydrogen smiled in understanding.

As they traveled, Julie fell into her now customary reverie. She discovered that she found it interesting—not funny—to see a horse smile. All of the Periodics had already exhibited many human traits, and smiling was no more surprising than curling up to sleep at night instead of grazing all night while asleep on their feet. Julie wondered where she had learned that fact about horses. She dimly recalled a library book titled *Horses: Our Equine Equals*.

"What time is it?" she asked suddenly.

"Somewhat after noon," replied Al, and Julie wondered where the time had gone. It seemed like only a few hours since morning. Then again, it *was* only a few hours.

They trotted down the dirt path, kicking up dust. Now Julie noticed that huge numbers were engraved into the steep cliffs and overhangs of Addition. As they passed a large "3" set into a smooth, red-brown rock face beside the path, Julie reached out to touch it. The engraving was about an inch deep and was as tall as Al.

They stopped for lunch half an hour later beside a cool stream which trickled off the mountain and fell, fell into Subtraction. It seemed to Julie that the water fell faster than normal, but was that possible? Also, it had a blue tinge to it, but Julie couldn't tell if this came from the liquid itself or the gravel beneath it, which also appeared blue.

"Heavy Water," commented Lithium, sniffing it.

"Excellent!" exclaimed Deuterium, showing some animation. "You're quite right," he said, lowering his nose toward the stream. "With a healthy supply of deuterium in it." He dropped down and dangled his hooves in the water.

"Is it safe to drink?" asked Julie plaintively. She was very thirsty, and the rain clouds overhead only made it worse.

"If I say so," Deuterium told her. "Drink away."

Julie sat next to the stream with a sigh and drank deeply of the cool, wet water.

"I think I'll have some myself," muttered Deuterium, lapping the water as if it were a fine wine. Hydrogen and the others also bent down for a drink, though they imbibed with a little less relish.

"That was very good," sighed Al, straightening at last. He swished his tail and looked around. "Let's all have some lunch, and then we can resume our travels." He nudged Julie gently, almost knocking her off her feet, and she clambered up onto his back.

"You don't know your own strength," she admonished him, as they cantered easily up a slope to where Al apparently scented fresh grass.

"Sorry about that," said Al, bending his ears back apologetically.

They came to the grass—a small mountain meadow—and stopped. Here the thick green turf was dotted with bright yellow flowers, and everything slanted slightly up the mountainside. The stream that had assuaged their thirst ran through the center, and the lush grasses bent over it. Julie threw herself down on the ground beside the stream and sighed. A breeze brushed her face and rustled the grass.

Julie was just taking out one cube of food when there was a light pitter-patter all around her and she felt small drops on her bare arms. Soon the rain began to fall heavily, making ripples in the stream and soaking the travelers.

"Well, at least I don't have to uncube the food," she sighed, shielding the two loaves of bread in her arms as they all ran for the nearest cover—a lone tree growing on the edge of the meadow, where grass met bare rock. The tree was very old and twisted, but its foliage spread far out and there was enough room for all of them beneath it without crowding. They stood watching the downpour soak the mountain for several minutes.

"What kind of tree is this, Al?" asked Julie, patting the rough bark gently, in a friendly way.

"I don't know," Al replied, "but it seems to me it's a pleasantree."

The others found that quite amusing, and they settled down for lunch under the tree in high spirits. Soon the rain passed and they emerged from beneath the tree, calling goodbye to it as they rode on.

They made very good time, and by nightfall Julie was quite sure that by tomorrow morning—noon at the latest—they would be out of the region of Subtraction and Addition. While the others talked quietly among themselves, she sat on an outcropping of rock, gazing over the rest of Addition toward the land beyond. It was too dark to make out any details, but it appeared to be more flat meadow, marked here and there by clumps of trees.

As she looked out into the night, she wondered what her parents and little brother were doing. Were they searching for her? Did they think something terrible had happened to her? She wanted to cry, but she held back her tears. She didn't want Al and the others to see.

7

The Wolframs Attack

BY MORNING THE SKY HAD CLEARED A LITTLE, BUT THERE were still some heavy thunderheads blocking the sun.

"Those clouds look rather unfriendly," said Tritium from beside Julie, gazing up into the sky.

"I'm sure they won't get us," Hydrogen assured him cheerfully.

Lithium snorted. "Didn't it rain enough yesterday?"

"The plants here need a lot of water," explained Hydrogen. "They need to make sure each one has enough."

Julie wondered who "they" were. The clouds? She didn't ask, however, because suddenly the path took a sharp turn upward.

"Why couldn't it just have gone straight?" she complained, as they laboriously climbed the grade.

"I wish I knew," grumbled Al, underneath her. "Maybe you should get off."

"Why?" Julie didn't mind walking a little distance, but she was curious. "Am I too heavy for you all of a sudden?"

"It's not that," Al answered, carefully stepping onto a small rock which looked loose. A small "5" was engraved on it. "With you on my back, my center of balance is off. I might fall."

"Oh, okay," said Julie, hopping down. She walked beside him, keeping a cautious hand on his white-and-black-marked neck. One of the equations that zig-zagged across his coat read "3 x 2 + 5n = rst."

"What does this equation mean?" inquired Julie, ruffling the fur around the area.

Al glanced down. "I don't know all of them," he said. "I think it's just a minor equation, one my father once used in a mathematical problem."

"Oh," said Julie. "How about this one?" She pulled gently at a tuft of fur beside "d = r x t."

"Now, I know that one," Al replied, glancing down again. "That stands for 'distance equals rate times time.'"

"Distance equals rate times time? How do you use it?"

"Well, let's say we went twenty-four miles yesterday. That was our 'distance.' It took us about eight hours. That was our 'time.' Distance equals rate times time, so rate equals distance divided by time. Okay? Same equation, just turned around. Twenty-four divided by eight is three. Our distance was twenty-four miles, our time was eight hours; therefore, our rate was three miles per hour."

"I don't think we went that slowly," said Julie doubtfully.

"Well, perhaps I don't have the distance right," Al said, cocking his ears in puzzlement. They were still going straight up the side of the mountain, all of them laboring now.

"Where is this crazy path taking us?" demanded Julie abruptly.

"Up," Deuterium told her.

Julie looked around. The scenery had changed. There was more plant life here, grass and trees and some small, fruit-bearing bushes. The trees looked much like normal trees, with brown trunks and ordinary leaves, except that both apples and oranges were growing on each.

Julie inspected the trees as they went past, bewildered. "Why are there apples and oranges on those trees?" she asked.

"Because three apples plus five oranges equal eight fruits," Al told her.

"What?" Julie was confused, but Al didn't reply.

Finally the path curved to the left and started heading down at a gentle slant, although the mountain itself was still as steep as ever. At a distance, away from the path and up the mountain, Julie spied a small herd of animals grazing. Both cows and deer were in the herd.

"What are they doing all mixed up?" she asked.

"Because four cows plus two deer equal six animals," Al recited.

"You're not making any sense, Al," she told him.

"Think back to kindergarten, Human," Al replied. "What did you use when learning to add?"

"Pictures of animals and fruit," Julie said, the light dawning. "Three fish plus one fish equal four fish. Two cats plus five dogs equal seven pets."

"Very good," approved Al. "Those are your pictures, right there."

"Don't worry about it," Deuterium assured her quickly. "Mathematics is hopelessly convoluted."

"No, I understand," Julie asserted, reaching out and patting him firmly. She looked at Al, wishing she could get back on and ride some more.

"Getting tired?" inquired Al, as if reading her mind. Julie gratefully accepted a boost from Lithium and climbed back on the gebra's back. She *was* a little fatigued. Going up the path had been strenuous exercise.

She sighed and held on with her legs as she let her mind wander. Cows and deer, oranges and apples. The group continued on down the path until Julie was sure they were well below the level they had been on before.

"Where is this path taking us?" she asked again, looking around. The walls of Subtraction rose up steeply on both sides, marked here and there with large numbers. They were winding their way down the side of the chasm, the path becoming cracked and dry the deeper they went.

"Down," Deuterium answered, with the same mocking succinctness as before.

"Very good, Deuterium," Lithium stated sarcastically. "I bet you know about left and right, too."

"Sure do," said Deuterium cheerfully.

"Okay, you two," Hydrogen said, to forestall an argument. "Let's just pick up the pace and see if we can't reach the end of this path's convolutions and level off again."

Julie mused about how mathematics, the subject, and Mathematics, the land, could both be convoluted. Somehow it all seemed to make sense.

They moved up to a fast trot, then a canter, and finally to a full gallop down the side of the valley. A cloud of dust drifted up behind them.

Julie looked around as they moved, adjusting herself easily now to each new gait, and noticed that the scenery in Subtraction was exactly the same as in Addition. A herd of cows and deer stampeded away from them as they passed their grazing point.

They were almost to the bottom of the valley, where the sunlight wasn't too strong and there were fewer herds and fruit trees. Julie had begun to worry that something might jump out at them in the dark—or that someone might stumble and fall—when suddenly the path leveled off for a bit, then started rising again. Everyone breathed a sigh of relief as they started to climb once more.

This time the path had apparently made up its mind, and it kept them on a basically level course—once they had reached their original elevation—although it wasn't very straight. Near the top, Julie saw a "24" engraved in a gray patch of red-brown rock, the largest number in quantity and size she had noticed so far.

Just before nightfall Julie could see, some miles in the distance, the end of the mountain and the broad plain beyond. "We're almost out," she announced, relieved, and settled down for dinner with a feeling of accomplishment.

As they fell asleep that night, Julie couldn't stop herself from thinking of home. She tried twisting on her side, pushing the thought firmly away and trying to think of other things, but again and again her family and home kept coming into her mind. She felt an aching loneliness and curled up against Hydrogen, seeking comfort. Tears ran down her face and Hydrogen tenderly licked them away.

"What's wrong?" the Periodic whispered, nuzzling her tangled hair.

"I miss my home and family," whimpered Julie, more tears running down her face.

"There, there," soothed Hydrogen gently, rocking back and forth on the ground with Julie. "You'll be all right. Soon you'll be home."

"I keep wondering what they're doing. I've been gone for almost a week!"

Hydrogen got the brush out of Al's saddlebag and ran it through her hair, using her mouth to hold it. Then they talked until Julie finally fell asleep, cuddled against the female Periodic's side.

In the morning as they walked, a chill breeze blew down the path, which was sometimes narrow, sometimes wide. Julie shivered. "It's getting colder," she said, and the others agreed.

"You, in your Human world, have ordinary seasons and months, but here we just have varying weather," Lithium informed her. "It seems today it will be like fall."

"And tomorrow, I guess, it will snow," sighed Julie. She wasn't dressed for cold, and shivered again. She needed a long-sleeved shirt.

"Take the blanket," Hydrogen told her, and Julie reached out gratefully to accept the warm woolen blanket.

About midday they came to the end of Addition and Subtraction, and stopped for one last meal in the Orders of Operations. Julie picked some apples and oranges from low-growing tree branches. Then they continued on. They all seemed to be in a hurry, having the end of their journey almost in sight.

"What is the Mathematician's Castle like?" Julie asked.

"You'll see, you'll see," Al told her. "Believe me, once you get there you'll learn anything you want to know and probably more."

"But what does the Castle look like?" she persisted.

"You'll see, you'll see."

When it was dark they stopped and built a campfire out on the wide plain. From far away came a weird, high-pitched howling.

"What's that?" demanded Julie, her hair standing on end.

"Wolframs," said Lithium nervously.

"Wolframs?" The cold wind had died down, but Julie shivered.

"Yes. They serve Tungsten."

"Tungsten? Who's he?"

"One of the Periodics. He's one of the rarer elements, and he's pretty nuts."

"How come he has servants and you don't?"

"He just does," said Hydrogen. "I don't know where he gets them."

"Will the Wolframs eat us?"

"I don't think so. I think they only eat wolframite."

"What's wolframite?"

"A type of mineral," Hydrogen told her. "The Wolframs love it."

"What do Wolframs look like?" asked Julie anxiously, edging close to the fire.

"Well, most of the time they look like shaggy brown wolves. But sometimes they change into large, powerful rams. A few live in Addition in ram form, though they stay away from the path between Addition and Subtraction."

"Will they come to the fire?"

"I don't think so. I think they're only telling us to stay away from their territories in Addition."

"But we've left Addition!"

"Yes, I know," Hydrogen said. Julie saw that the Periodic was shivering. Al and the others seemed anxious and edgy.

"Why do you all look so nervous?" That in itself made Julie uneasy.

"I don't think they'll bother us," Hydrogen comforted her, coming close. "They're somewhat intelligent." She settled down to sleep, nibbling delicately at some grass within her reach.

"Yes, somewhat," Lithium agreed, easing himself down onto the ground beside the fire. Al did the same on Julie's other side.

"Still . . . " began Deuterium, and Tritium nodded, even though Deuterium didn't finish his sentence.

"Good, you two get first watch," Lithium told them, chuckling in a low voice. He chomped on some grass, then closed his eyes and began to snore softly, which surprised Julie.

She gradually dozed off, lulled by the warmth of the fire and the sight of the wide black sky above, strewn with bright points of starlight.

Around midnight she was suddenly awakened by a fierce stomping and wild noise. Hydrogen was gone, and Al lay beside her with an intent look on his face. Lithium was just outside the circle of light, squealing and stomping ferociously. All around there was a fearsome howling, which sounding eerily like "Human, Human!"

"What's going on?" she asked, sitting up, but Al swished his tail, silencing her.

"Go away! Leave!" Lithium let out a fierce squeal and half-reared up on his hind legs, coming down with a loud stomp. A large, dark shadow leaped out of the way just in time. Its glowing green-yellow eyes sent terror down Julie's spine.

"Human!" came the spooky cry, fading into the distance. "Human, Human!"

"Get out of here!" cried Hydrogen, galloping up from the side. "Awful animals!"

"What's going on?" demanded Julie, frightened.

"Wolframs," Al explained. "They decided to come see what was up. They're going now."

Hydrogen turned her head to talk with Tritium, who had just come into the circle of light. "Everything all right?"

"We managed to drive them back. They sure seemed curious about something."

"More than curious," put in Lithium, coming to stand beside her. "I had to give two of them a good solid kick before they decided to leave."

"Um," agreed Deuterium, appearing from the other side. "Human."

"Why did they want me?"

"Do you remember that talk we had about the powers Humans have?" asked Al. "Well, the Wolframs didn't know you were so young. They thought you were one of the mathematicians or scientists the Mathematician sometimes imports to help keep order. If Tungsten could get his hooves on one of those Humans, he could—" Al broke off.

"He could what?"

"He could be powerful. Very powerful." Al didn't seem to think that was such an excellent idea.

Julie was puzzled and frightened, but the Periodics and the Isotopes and the gebra lay down around her, and she slowly fell back into a light, uneasy sleep.

$$\{3[3+(2\times6)]\}+[4(13-6)]=$$

In the morning it was warm again. Julie stretched, feeling the sun on her stomach, and sat up.

"Glorious morning," Al greeted her.

"Yes, it is." She grinned at him and stretched again. "What's for breakfast?"

"Looks like more barometer berries," said Hydrogen, getting them out of the pack. "We forgot to use them up on Addition mountain."

"How do they work, Deu?" Tritium asked, sniffing them.

"The higher you get, the bluer they become," explained Deuterium.

Hydrogen gave Julie the berries, holding in her mouth the small branch they were still attached to.

"They're a little soft," Julie said, munching on the sweet berries. "But they're okay."

She had a mouth full of berries and juice on her chin when all at once a tall, thin man rode up on a prancing horse. The horse's bridle and saddle were trimmed with gold, and an emerald green blanket was underneath the saddle.

"And who," demanded the man, "are you?"

8

At the Mathematician's Castle

WITHOUT WAITING FOR AN ANSWER, THE MAN CLIMBED DOWN from his horse and gazed superciliously at each of them, as if he were inspecting them. He was dressed in a long white robe trimmed in yellow-gold fur. His short brown hair was touched with gray.

"You are journeying to the Castle?" he inquired, directing the question at Lithium.

"Yes, we are," replied Lithium. "And who are *you*?"

"I am the Human Mark Carscian," the tall man said haughtily.

"Good for you," Lithium answered.

Hydrogen nudged him. "Show a little respect," she murmured tensely.

"Have you come in contact with any Wolframs?" asked the man.

"As a matter of fact, they bothered us last night," Lithium answered.

"Are you carrying any wolframite?"

"Of course not."

"Do you have amongst you any sample of the element tungsten?"

"Absolutely not!" exclaimed Lithium. "We know the danger."

"Then I suppose there's no need for me to search your packs," stated Mark, relaxing a bit but still eyeing them suspiciously.

"You can search them if you like," said Al indifferently. He was lying in front of Julie, shielding her from the man's sight. Now he stood up.

"If you're that willing, I suppose it isn't necessary." Mark's eyes widened as he saw Julie for the first time. "And who is this?"

"I'm Julie," she answered quickly, standing and brushing the grass and dirt from her jeans and straightening her hair. She held out a hand.

"Pleased to meet you," said Mark, looking at her suspiciously. He shook her hand uncertainly. "I am Mark, a Human."

"Well, I am Julie, a Human too." She smiled good-naturedly. "And this is Al, the gebra; Lithium and Hydrogen, the Periodics; and Deuterium and Tritium, Hydrogen's Isotope-brothers."

"Greetings," Mark said, glancing at each in turn as Julie introduced them. Then he turned back to Julie. "Another Human! I didn't know you were here. When did you arrive, and how long do you plan to stay?"

"Well, actually, I'm lost," admitted Julie, sighing. "I'm going to the Castle to see if I can get a little help."

"I see," said the man. "An Accident-Crosser."

"A what?"

"Someone who came to Mathematics by accident. It happens fairly often, but most get pulled back into their world after a few hours or days. How long have you been here?"

"About a week." Julie felt another surge of homesickness well up inside her.

"A week! That's very rare!" Mark took a few steps back and inspected her again. "Are you sure you're a Human?"

"Two plus two is four," stated Julie, smiling winningly. From what she had learned, that was all she needed to do to prove her human "powers."

"Well, I suppose you are Human," said Mark under his breath. Then he raised his voice: "Well, then, if you'll all follow me back to the Castle, I'll guarantee you a quick audience with the Mathematician."

They got underway and went at a fast trot across the wide plain, following Mark's brown steed.

"Is that a real horse?" Julie asked, urging Al to pull up beside the man. "Al, here, told me that the closest relatives he had in Mathematics were the Periodics, and he'd never heard of a horse."

"Your friend is correct," Mark replied, patting his steed's neck. "He's just an image of a horse."

"Then how can you ride him?"

"He's really an Imaginary Number."

That brought Julie back to reality hard and fast. "I was following an Imaginary Number when I ended up here!" she exclaimed. "He visited me in my room."

"Making house calls, eh? Must be an amateur. Don't worry. We'll get you straightened out."

Julie waved at Mark's steed. "Hello, there," she said in a friendly voice. It snorted in return. Since the last time Julie had seen an Imaginary Number, she had learned a lot. It was best to be nice to them.

"How far is it to the Mathematician's Castle?" she asked curiously.

"About half a day's travel," replied Mark.

"We must have gone farther yesterday than we thought," mused Lithium out loud. "I thought it would be at least another day and a half."

"No, we're going on the Highway," Mark told them.

"The Highway! That's only for official Mathematician business!"

"This *is* official Mathematician business. You're with me."

"Oh, that explains everything," sighed Al. "We're with him, so it's official."

They came to a wide sheet of concrete, running from left to right as far as the eye could see across the meadow. "This is the Highway," Mark announced importantly.

"We might have guessed," Lithium muttered. The Highway seemed to shimmer in the sun, as if a layer of silvery blue gauze hovered just a few inches above it. They stepped with some trepidation onto the smooth path.

"I'm not sure how to walk on this," stated Deuterium nervously. "Please tell me." He swished his tail uneasily and crowded next to Tritium, who pressed against Hydrogen.

"It's easy," spoke up Mark's steed, surprising Julie. She had almost forgotten that he was an Imaginary Number and, therefore, could speak if he wanted to. "You just walk normally. But your speed will be double what it usually is."

"Okay," conceded Deuterium, nodding politely. He still looked uncertain.

They set off down the Highway at a brisk trot, and indeed the scenery flew past.

"It looks like we're going more than double our normal speed," Julie observed. "Maybe three times faster is more like it."

"Well, I rounded it off for the science beings," explained the Imaginary Number horse.

"Excuse me, good Imaginary Number," Lithium broke in. "We are Periodics and Isotopes—and a gebra," he said, nodding toward Al. "We are not, as you put it, 'science beings.'" Lithium sounded somewhat affronted but still respectful.

"You are beings of science. That is enough."

Julie could almost see Lithium thinking, "Now, what does he mean by 'that is enough?'"

They soon came to a fork in the road where a large sign read, "LEFT TO MATHEMATICIAN'S CASTLE, RIGHT TO REGION OF SCIENCE."

"Let's turn right," suggested Deuterium. "The Human Mark can bring the girl to the Mathematician without us."

"Why, Deu!" exclaimed Tritium. "Julie is our friend! I won't abandon her until she reaches her destination."

"Yes, I know she's our friend. It's just that . . . well, the Mathematician . . . ." Deuterium swished his tail back and forth several times in agitation.

"He doesn't bite," put in the Imaginary Number horse.

"Yes, I know, but . . . ."

"If he makes you nervous, we can wait outside," Tritium comforted his Isotope-brother.

"Yes, that would be good," agreed Deuterium.

The Imaginary Number snorted.

As for Julie, she was not feeling very sure herself about meeting this King of Math. "What is he like?" she inquired of Mark.

"He is very powerful. You must not insult him, and you must show proper respect." Mark glanced quickly at Lithium.

"Do you think he'll let me go home?"

"I'm pretty sure. He's a kindhearted man."

"He's a human?"

"Oh, yes, I believe he is Human," Mark nodded. "And he will help you, I'm positive. What grades do you get in math at school?"

"C's," admitted Julie, leaving out the "and D's" that would be the whole truth. "I'm taking Algebra One."

"Ah, yes. I remember my first year of algebra in school."

"What did you get?"

"All A's, of course!" Mark laughed out loud. "To me, it sounds as if you need a tutor."

"Oh, I'll get along somehow." Julie smiled warmly at him, inwardly writhing. Actually, the last thing she wanted was to waste any more time on her algebra homework than was absolutely necessary. A tutor would extend that time to an hour or even longer.

They stopped for a quick lunch, and Julie ate some sandwiches that Mark had brought along. She was pleasantly surprised to find that they were made of peanut butter and barometer-berry jelly.

After a few minutes' travel down the road, they spotted a tall spire on the horizon, looking like Addition Mountain when it had first appeared. But this spire was thinner and shone a bright white. An hour later, they were standing before the solid gate of an ornate fence that ran all the way around the base of the structure.

Julie looked up and up, past the thick gates she suspected were made of gold alloy, until she got dizzy. Far, far up, not as high as Addition but high enough, she saw the tip-top of the tower. Every 30 feet or so there was a thick black line and a number. Julie found herself thinking of a humongous ruler.

"Hello and welcome to the Mathematician's Castle," the guard at the gate greeted them. "As you can see, the structure reaches 100 meters into the sky. It has 20 levels, each 5 meters high. Every two levels there is a black mark which indicates a new section. The castle was built—"

"Okay, cut the tourist performance," Mark interrupted the gatekeeper. "We're here on official business."

Julie remembered what Al had told her when she asked what the castle was like: "You'll learn anything you want to know and probably more." That was certainly true so far.

"I'll send a message inside immediately," said the gate-keeper briskly. He pushed some buttons inside his little house, which was just to one side of the gate.

"How long will it be before the Mathematician can see us?" Julie inquired anxiously.

"He can probably see you from an upper level already," the gatekeeper told her.

"She means how long before he can *take an audience,* stupid," Mark snapped at him.

Julie looked at him, astonished. That was not a nice way to speak to anyone!

"Oh. In just a few minutes, sir," the gatekeeper replied meekly.

"Thank you. Now, how about letting us in?"

The gate swung open soundlessly and they all walked through—even Deuterium, who was too awed and curious to be frightened.

Once they were inside the golden gates and crossing the courtyard, Mark turned to them. Keeping his voice low, he confided, "That gatekeeper has been getting on my nerves for years."

Julie glanced down at the clean white courtyard. She saw that it was made of neat white tiles, probably cut from some kind of rock, since her friends' hooves rang loudly against it. As she inspected the tiles more closely, she saw that each had a different number engraved on it—"36," "25," "16," and others. The same numbers were repeated over and over.

"What are they?" She pointed at the tiles.

"I believe they are pure quartz," Mark replied, gazing down. "Imported from Addition."

"They are all so perfectly square."

"Of course," Mark said. "They are Perfect Squares." He laughed and looked down at the tiles fondly.

"I don't get it," said Julie, puzzled.

"Perfect Squares? And you don't get it?" Mark smiled at her, still laughing.

"No," replied Julie testily, feeling that she was being teased.

"Haven't you ever heard of a perfect square trinomial? No? Then how about a perfect square binomial? Not that, either?" Mark shook his head as Julie shook hers. "They must come later in your math book than you've gotten."

"That's probably it," Julie assented, still wondering about the joke. What was a perfect square, anyway—in mathematical terms?

"A perfect square is a number you get from squaring an integer," Al whispered to her.

"You mean multiplying something by itself twice?" Julie perked up.

"By itself once," asserted Mark, glancing sidelong at her and Al.

"Like seven times seven equals forty-nine," Al said. "Forty-nine is a perfect square."

"Oh!" Julie looked down at the tiles in amusement. Mark grinned to himself, shaking his head.

They passed through a pair of heavy wooden doors buttressed with deep gray metal and entered a high hall. At the far end was a tall, narrow window of stained glass, and running down both sides were thick white columns which did not reflect light. Overall, the room was rather dim. Suits of armor and other old-castle paraphernalia stood in the crannies formed by the columns, which were spaced about every seven feet or so.

Against the back wall below the window was a platform, and on the platform was a throne. Between the window and the throne was a wide banner decorated with all kinds of mathematical equations, symbols, and statements. On the throne sat a white, wrinkled man.

9

Julie Goes Home

LIKE THE FENCE THAT ENCIRCLED THE CASTLE, THE Mathematician's throne also appeared to be made of gold. As they slowly drew nearer, Julie saw that the Mathematician's long, narrow white beard and mustache hung down over his deep blue robe, which was monogrammed with an "M" in fancy writing. The robe was trimmed with white fur, which mingled with his beard and fell to his feet. A small, simple crown of medium-gray metal was set upon his head.

Julie climbed off of Al's back. Al nickered to her gently as she walked slowly down the rest of the length of the hall. The gebra, the Periodics, and the Isotopes stayed near the wooden doors, but Mark and the Imaginary Number horse followed a few steps behind her. Julie went all the way up to the platform upon which the throne rested. She stopped and waited quietly, keeping her eyes on the platform. She felt like bowing, but girls were supposed to curtsy, and she didn't know how to do that.

"Hello, little girl," said the Mathematician kindly. He stood up from his throne and came toward her, stepping down from the platform. Julie saw that he was quite short, his head barely reaching to her chest. He held out his hand.

"Hello," Julie said shyly. She timidly took the proffered hand. Despite his somewhat frail appearance, the Mathematician's grip was firm.

"What brings you to my castle?"

"Well, actually, I'm lost," began Julie. "You see, I came through a portal, and then I didn't go back through it, and couldn't even remember where it was, and I went to the Elemental Forest—"

"Hold on, hold on," the old man interrupted, raising both hands and trying not to smile. "Let us sit down, and then we can hear this story. I've a feeling it will be a long one." He drew her to an alcove between two columns, where a short table had been prepared for two. They sat across from each other on wooden chairs. Julie wasn't surprised to see that the chairs were carved with mathematical equations. Some of the equations were starting to look familiar.

The table was set with square, grid-marked plates, round napkins, two tea cups, and a plate of cookies—chocolate-chip, Julie thought, but she couldn't be sure until she tasted one.

"Would you like a cookie?" asked the Mathematician, smiling. "And some tea?"

"Oh, yes," Julie answered gratefully. She rarely drank tea at home, but chocolate-chip cookies were her favorite snack, and just the sight of them made her feel better, as if she really might be able to go home soon.

As Julie reached for a cookie, Mark whispered something in the Mathematician's ear. The old man nodded, and Mark and his Imaginary Number companion left, their footfalls echoing down the hall. Julie watched them go. When she turned back to the table, her cup was brimming with light brown tea, steam curling over the edge. There was no sign of a teapot. The Mathematician winked at her startled look.

"Now, how did you get to our land in the first place?" prompted the old man, watching her intensely. Julie was nervous, but his demeanor was still friendly, so she forced herself to relax.

"Well, I followed an Imaginary Number—"

"Aha! One of the Numbers. Now I am beginning to understand. It talked to you, did it not?"

"Well, yes. It criticized me for being bad in math, and I wanted to talk to it some more, so I ran after it—"

"Ah, yes. That happens a lot. And according to Mark, you say you can't return home?"

"That's right."

"Well, let me get that Imaginary Number in here—I'll need his report—and I'll set about working out the intricate equation necessary for your transportation back."

"Oh, thank you!" exclaimed Julie, standing up and throwing her arms impulsively around the old man's neck.

"Ah, child, it's nothing," laughed the Mathematician. "It's been a long time since one so young has visited me here." He summoned an Imaginary Number, which instantly appeared at his side. Julie studied it carefully. It wasn't her Imaginary Number—its features were different, dim and fuzzy as they were.

"I want to see the Number who made contact with this child," the Mathematician instructed. Then he turned to Julie. "Which one did you say it was?"

Julie was at a loss. "I never caught his name. It all happened so fast, and I just—"

"Of course! How silly of me! Bromius, just check the records. What's your full name, dear?"

"Julie Alicia Polray, Your Majesty."

"Sh, sh," the old man told her, waving her down. "'Your Majesty' indeed. Goodness, child!" He laughed, patting her on the back. Bromius the Imaginary Number left, making a note on a piece of paper. "He'll be a while. In the meantime, I'll let your friends enjoy a good meal in one of my pastures. They'll find samples of their elements there, whatever they may be." He turned toward the wooden doors, where Al, Lithium, Hydrogen, Deuterium, and Tritium were waiting apprehensively. "Tell one of my servants to guide you to my best pasture," he called to them. "The Human will be safe with me." He turned back to Julie. "And now we'll see about getting you home." Julie's friends left, and the doors closed behind them.

About half an hour later, an Imaginary Number entered. Julie recognized the translucent cloud as the Number that had started her on her journey.

"Oh, Jerion! I should have known." The Mathematician slapped his forehead suddenly. "I apologize most sincerely, Human Julie. Jerion here is just a rookie. Been sneaking around in Humans' bedrooms, eh, Jerion?"

"That girl!" exclaimed Jerion, pointing one fuzzy white extremity at her. "What is she doing here?"

"She came here. She followed you through the portal, and she has been trapped here ever since." The Mathematician shook his finger at the Imaginary Number, which suddenly looked mortified. "And you didn't even make a note of it on our Lost Humans list!"

"I am truly sorry, Mathematician. It won't happen again."

"There, there," stated the Mathematician, waving him away. "It was your first week on the job, and we all make mistakes. Now, what exactly happened?"

Jerion the Imaginary Number recounted the whole story, from Julie's screaming the "horribly incorrect algebra problem" in her dream, to the moment when he confronted her in her room, to Julie's declaration that "she hates math," to his sudden departure. "I knew she followed me," Jerion explained, "but I had heard that most Humans get pulled back into their world within a few hours. I really am sorry. I thought—"

"Well, most do get pulled back," interrupted the Mathematician. "But now you know that you're supposed to report any real Humans you bring into Mathematics." The Mathematician paused and winked humorously at the downcast Imaginary Number. "Unless, of course, you thought Julie wasn't a real Human. Somehow I don't think she'd agree." He stopped and chuckled, then continued, "Now, the only thing left to do is to send her home."

"I wonder what my family has thought, with me being gone," Julie said. "I bet they've been worried. Maybe they think something terrible has happened to me."

"Oh, we can fix it so you return home only an hour after you left," the Mathematician reassured her, patting her on the back. "Time, like algebra, is just a series of equations. Everything will be all right. You'll see. Do you trust me?"

Julie nodded, her hopes rising. She had made a lot of good friends here, but she was anxious to get home.

"Now, this is going to take a few hours," the Mathematician warned her. "You may stay here, or we'll find a room for you until I'm ready." He gathered up his blue robe and hurried out of the room by a doorway to the left of the throne.

Julie looked at the Imaginary Number. "Will you stay with me?" she asked. The Number nodded, or what passed for a nod. They talked for a while, getting to know each other better. She told him all about her adventures in Mathematics, which he responded to sympathetically, and she realized that he wasn't so bad after all.

"It was just my first week," he apologized. "I'm sorry if I seemed abrupt and haughty with you."

"Oh, it's okay," Julie sighed. "Soon I'll be home." She smiled at him. Then an idea came to her. "Do you have any paper around here? And a pencil?"

"Sure, lots. Why?"

"Well," she replied, "if I have a few hours free, I'm going to work on my story."

"You're writing a story?" The Imaginary Number seemed filled with awe as he fetched several sheets of lined paper and a pencil from beneath the throne. "About what?"

Julie sighed. "That's the problem. I can't seem to get started."

She smoothed the paper with one hand, sitting at the table, and sighed again. She tried to start the writing process by making a brainstormed list, free-writing, and even drawing a cluster, but nothing helped. Whenever she began to write, she got all tangled up.

"I need a really good topic," she said. "Something that I can write fast, because the due date is next week, but it has to be good, too."

"Nonfiction or fiction?" inquired Jerion curiously.

"Fiction, if I could ever think of something to write."

"How about your adventures here? That's really non-fiction, but no one would ever believe—"

"What?" asked Julie, sitting up very straight. "That's a wonderful idea!" She grabbed her pencil and began to write furiously.

"I'm glad I could be of some help," Jerion told her. "After all, I was the one who got you into this mess."

"That's why I'm going to dedicate my story to you," Julie declared, making a large note on the top page.

"Why, thank you," exclaimed the Imaginary Number. "I've never had anything dedicated to me!" Julie just smiled and continued scribbling.

Time passed. After an hour—it might have been longer—the Mathematician returned.

"I've got the equation," he announced. "Come, dear Julie." He motioned her near, then turned to the Imaginary Number. "Jerion, go get her companions, if you please."

As Jerion hurried out, the Mathematician laid an arm over Julie's shoulders and brought his face close to hers.

"Since you stayed here so long," he murmured confidentially, "I might as well warn you about a facet of our land you may not be aware of. You see," he said, shifting his arm, "since you are a Human, you have certain . . . *powers* . . . in our land that the denizens do not. I'm sure you've already heard this from your friends."

Julie nodded.

"Well," the Mathematician went on, "the longer you stay in Mathematics, the more . . . *focused* . . . those powers become. You have already been here a week, and were you to stay any longer, your powers would begin fully functioning after a few more days. That's why it's important to hurry you out of here. We're in troubled times, Julie, and we have an enemy that can lock on to persons of power. You would have become a target very soon, and his Wolframs would have come for you."

Gasping, Julie relayed what had happened the night before. The Mathematician looked grim. "Well, this is not your problem. You are going home, right?" He smiled weakly and handed her a piece of paper.

Equations literally covered both sides of it, scribbled sideways, upside down, and in every other direction. The Mathematician looked slightly sheepish.

"I never was a neat writer," he said. "But it works." He started to step back from her, then seemed to change his mind.

"One more thing," he said. "Our land is conducive to learning and understanding mathematics—or science, depending on where you are. You may have found yourself able to comprehend concepts you wouldn't ordinarily have understood. I'd just like to warn you that anything you have learned here will follow you into your world. Most likely, you will do much better in your math studies for quite a while. Forever, if you choose to take part of our land with you." He shrugged. "Pick up a rock, if you like." He beamed at her.

Just then they heard a clatter in the courtyard. The doors opened, and Al, Lithium, Hydrogen, Deuterium, and Tritium appeared. Side by side, they approached Julie, looking sad.

"Are you leaving?" asked Tritium woefully.

"I'm afraid so," Julie responded. "I need to go home." She rustled the Mathematician's paper in her hands.

"Will you ever be back?" asked Al.

"Oh, I'm sure I will." She glanced at the Mathematician to see how he took this news, but he was shuffling back toward his throne. "In the meantime, Al, I intend to do as well in your subject as I can."

Al the gebra smiled. "Here," he said, taking an object from Hydrogen and giving it to her. "This is a charm to help you do just that."

"What is it?" she asked, turning it over in her hands. It appeared to be a link of braided hair.

"It's a braid of my tail, from the hair at the tassel. Keep it for luck. It will help you to understand algebra better." Julie smiled and threw her arms around his thick, furry neck.

"Oh, Al," she sighed. "I promise I'll get an A, or I'll come right back for proper help!"

"Well, in that case, don't get an A," stated Al brokenly, backing away slowly. Tears shone in his bright brown eyes.

Lithium came next, wordlessly handing her a small box made of dark gray metal.

"What is this?" Julie wanted to know.

"Inside is some pure lithium," the Periodic explained. "You must promise never to open the box, though, because lithium is a very reactive element. It will burn on contact with water, even with the humidity in the air."

Julie turned the box over. It seemed to have no latch. On the top was engraved the chemical symbol "Li" and the figure of a running horse—rather, a running Periodic. She wondered where Lithium had gotten such a wonderful gift, but she was too overwhelmed with emotion to ask.

Hydrogen, Deuterium, and Tritium nuzzled her and apologized for not being able to give her anything.

"Our elements are naturally gas, and besides, my element is radioactive," Tritium apologized. "But you know we'll always be with you."

Julie nodded and kissed each one of her friends, gave Hydrogen an extra hug, then turned to the Mathematician.

"I'm ready," she said.

The Mathematician smiled and nodded. "Then invoke the equation," he instructed. As Julie gave him a blank look, he explained, "On your paper is written the equation for your transportation home, plus a small warp of time. If you invoke it, it will go into operation and do what it is supposed to. Simply say, 'I invoke you.'"

Julie took one final look at each of her friends. Then she gathered up the pages of her story and proclaimed, "Equation for Transportation and Time Warping, I invoke you!"

$$\{3^{[3+(2\times6)]}\}+[4(13-6)]=$$

Julie abruptly found herself back in her room. There was no flash, no explosion, no streaks of light or colored laser beams. In her hands were the box Lithium had given her, the small braid of hair from Al, and the first few pages of her story. She was seated at her desk, and in front of her were her algebra book and her memo notebook.

The clock on her desk said 6:00. Her parents would be home by 6:30. She glanced out the window; it was still raining. The Mathematician was right. She had spent several days in the land of Mathematics, but in terms of the human world, she had been gone for about an hour. It felt good to be home again.

Julie placed her story pages to one side of her desk, with Lithium's box on top of them for a paperweight. Then she decided to experiment with her new good-luck charm. Holding it tightly in one hand, she opened her algebra book to the right page and began to work on her homework. To her surprise, she could comprehend the problems! When she came to the fourth problem, $7 + 4(3)$, she knew that she had to multiply the four and the three before she added the seven. That was because, in the order of operations, multiplication always came before addition.

Julie finished her homework quickly, set it aside, and turned to her story. She was confident now that it would be finished by next week's deadline, and she was already looking forward to finding out what the contest judges thought of it. She read what she had written on the top page: "To Jerion, the Imaginary Number." Above her dedication, she wrote the title: *A Gebra Named Al.*

About the Author

Wendy Isdell began writing her first book, *A Gebra Named Al,* when she was in the eighth grade. She entered the story in the Virginia Young Author's Contest of 1989, where it won first place in the Rappahannock regional competition and went on to capture first place at the state level. She sent her story to Free Spirit Publishing in 1992, and it was published in 1993, when Wendy was a senior in high school.

Scientific and mathematical information contained in this book was gathered from several classes Wendy took over the years, including Advanced Physical Science and Algebra 1 and 2; advanced classes in Earth Science, Chemistry, Geometry, Trigonometry, and Analytical Geometry; and Advanced Placement Chemistry.

Wendy recently earned her bachelor's degree in Creative Studies from a private university. She enjoys playing her guitar, hanging out with friends, and talking to her plants. Her eventual goal is to make enough of a living from her writing to support herself.

Other Great Books from Free Spirit

School Power
Study Skill Strategies for Succeeding in School
Revised and Updated Edition
by Jeanne Shay Schumm, Ph.D.
This popular study-skills handbook, newly revised and updated, covers everything students need to know, including how to get organized, take notes, do Internet research, write better, read faster, study smarter, follow directions, handle long-term assignments, and more. For ages 11 & up.
$16.95; 144 pp.; softcover; illus.; 8½" x 11"

The Teenagers' Guide to School Outside the Box
by Rebecca Greene
This practical, inspiring book explores the world of alternative learning, giving teens the knowledge and tools they need to make good choices. Rebecca Greene introduces and describes a world of possibilities, from study abroad to internships, apprenticeships, networking, job shadowing, service learning, and many more. For ages 13 & up.
$15.95; 272 pp.; softcover; illus.; 6" x 9"

Write Where You Are
How to Use Writing to Make Sense of Your Life
by Caryn Mirriam-Goldberg, Ph.D.
This insightful book helps teens articulate and understand their hopes and fears, lives and possibilities through writing. Not just another writing skills book, it invites teens to make sense of their lives through writing—and shows them how. Recommended for young writers, English teachers, and writing instructors. For ages 12 & up.
$14.95; 168 pp.; softcover; illus.; 7¼" x 9"

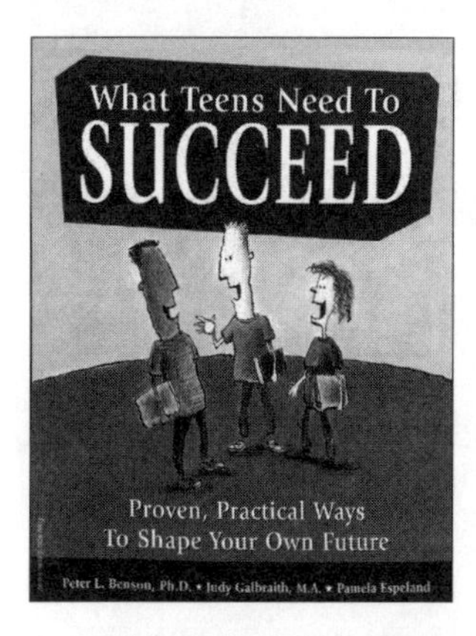

What Teens Need to Succeed
Proven, Practical Ways
to Shape Your Own Future
by Peter L. Benson, Ph.D., Judy Galbraith, M.A., and Pamela Espeland
Based on a national survey, this book describes 40 developmental "assets" all teens need to succeed in life, then gives hundreds of suggestions teens can use to build assets at home, at school, in the community, in the congregation, with friends, and with youth organizations. For ages 11 & up.
$15.95; 368 pp.; softcover; illus.; 7¼" x 9¼"

**They Broke the Law—
You Be the Judge**
True Cases of Teen Crime
by Thomas A. Jacobs, J.D.
Teens often hear about other teens who get into trouble with the law. But they're seldom asked what they think should happen next and why. This book invites teens to preside over a variety of real-life cases. Readers learn each teen's background, the relevant facts, and the sentencing options available. After deciding on a sentence, they find out what really happened—and where each offender is today. Thought-provoking and eye-opening, this book is for all teens who want to know more about the juvenile justice system and the laws that pertain to them and their peers. For ages 12 & up.
$15.95; 224 pp.; softcover; 6" x 9"